HE'S MY THUG, I'M HIS PEACE

THERESA REESE

Cole Hart
SIGNATURE NOVELS

He's My Thug, I'm His Peace

Mailing List

To stay up to date on new releases, plus get information on contests, sneak peeks, and more,

Go To The Website Below...

www.colehartsignature.com

FOREWORD

Texting List

To stay up to date on new releases, plus get information on contests, sneak peeks, and more...

Text ColeHartSig to (855)231-5230

1

LOU

"When something seems too perfect, usually some shit is about to pop off! No one lives in a perfect world."

"I can't believe this shit!" Gritting my teeth, I jumped up from the open drawer on the desk in the office that belonged to my fiancé. The white brick packaged in a clear wrapping stared back at me. Pacing back and forth across the dark-brown, sheepskin rug, I looked from the window to the door.

"This nigga been playing with me for the past three years," I mumble to no one in particular, looking at the ceiling. Trying to bring myself back down to zero, I couldn't help but think he was out here running the streets without a care in the world.

I was engaged to the pastor of the Baptist Calvary church in North Carolina; not that him being a pastor made a difference right now according to the bullshit he had been up to. Hassel was what you would call a good guy. Graduated college, no kids, no ex-wives and no ties to the streets. At thirty-three, he was doing great for himself. We lived in a five bedroom, three bathroom, fully furnished townhouse in Raleigh. Living with him was definitely a secret to the family, there was no way I was supposed to be shacking up before marriage, but whatever. *Shit happens.*

"Lucy!" I heard him calling my name with the deep voice he inherited from his father. I roll my eyes so hard I felt them in the top of my head before squeezing them tightly. Walking swiftly to the door, I drew it back, quickly hoping he didn't question me being there. That was one room that was off limits to me, just as my self-care room was to him. Hearing his hard bottom Giuseppe's across the hardwood floors, I stopped halfway through the hallway to meet him.

Placing my hands on my hips and tapping my foot impatiently, he walked up to me, dismissing my obvious attitude. Smirking, he planted a kiss on my forehead.

"Hassel, we need to talk honey," I said, being modest although I was fuming on the inside.

"Lucy it can wait, service starts soon and you aren't even fully dressed." He looked down at my clothing. My white, button-down shirt was open, exposing my nude colored bra. My burgundy pencil skirt was hiked up over my knees, which was a no go for him.

"It can't wait, I'm telling you right now if you walk away from me Hassel you can consider this engagement off!" Raising my soft voice higher than I would have liked, I turn on my heels and he threw his hands up in the air.

"Lucy, if that's what you want to do then do it. I'm tired of you threatening to end our engagement reese over bullshit!"

Fed up with his lack of compassion for my emotions, I walked up on him. Placing my manicured finger in his face, I explained to him that I was onto his secrets he thought he hid.

"What are you talking about Lucy?" Cocking his head to the side, he squinted his already chinky eyes. Slapping him across his face, I saw the shocked look in his eyes. Hassel was dark skinned, stood about six foot three inches and weighed over two hundred pounds. My petite frame stood no match for him, but I knew he was raised not to hit women.

"Hass, you really thought it wasn't going to get out that you're the man supplying the drugs to the community!" He shook his head, running his hand over his clean shaven face. "How can you claim you're cleaning the community if you're the one bringing the dirt here?" Jumping at him with emphasis, I was vexed. This couldn't be the man I accepted the proposal from. Hassel was the man of my dreams. My father approved of him, which didn't come easy because he felt no one was good enough for me.

"Lucy, you're blowing this out of proportion, you think I can afford all this shit?" Stopping short, he looked around our fully furnished house. "This shit doesn't get bought on the salary of a pastor. Them Gucci purses and that brand new BMW 3 Series you're riding around in came from my dealings."

Smacking my lips, I sighed heavily before turning around to leave him standing where he was. My curls had dropped as the sweat fuzzed up my once slicked edges. *I can't believe I figured I wouldn't get caught up in this life marrying a pastor,* I thought, entering our master bedroom. Slamming the door shut, I stomped over to the closet where my casual clothing hung. Rummaging through the dresses, I found something to change into. The perspiration under my arms and in between my caramel colored breasts made me huff.

The bedroom door swung open as Hassel walked in with his jaw clenched. "Lucy, cut the dramatic shit and let's go; you know it's the first Sunday of the month!" Ignoring his anger I slumped my shoulders, walking into the bathroom to proceed to a quick shower. He was shouting something through the locked bathroom door that I tuned out. Cutting on the shower and the sink water; I needed him to get out of my head. If I was going to put up a front in front of all these church people, then I might as well look amazing doing so.

Thirty minutes later, I stepped out of the bathroom feeling refreshed. Running my hands through my now wet dirty blonde tight curls, I pulled them up into a messy bun. With the towel tightly wrapped around my body, I sashayed into the bedroom. Feeling Hassel's eyes on my body, I sighed, hoping he would leave me alone.

"Luc, c'mon now, you trippin' fa'real." He tried to reach out and grab my arm. Moving away, he had to catch himself from losing his balance. This dude had never talked in this manner before and I see discovering his secret made him feel comfortable enough to be himself.

"I'll be down in about fifteen minutes." Grabbing the burgundy, form fitting dress that stopped just above my knee and black pumps, I walked back into the bathroom. Slipping my petite frame into my thong and bra set, I looked in the mirror admiring my figure. Petite yet shapely, slim waist, hips, thighs, just the right size of ass and small c-cup breasts. Yeah, I lacked in the breast area, but I made up for it elsewhere. Picking up the small, polka-dot makeup bag I owned, I applied the honey colored foundation and rose color blush. Brushing the mascara through my long lashes, I smiled at my reflection. My almond-shaped, dark-brown eyes were complimented by a few freckles on my nose. The beauty mark above the right side of my lips always attracted guys to my face.

"All set," I mouthed.

"Lucy, I'll be in the car!" Hearing Hassel's voice caused me to groan. Not in the mood to answer, I unlocked the bathroom door. Catching up to his stride in the foyer, I grabbed my small purse from the coat hook. Mumbling a bunch of nothings to no one in particular, I brushed past him unlocking my car door.

"We aren't riding in your car, Lucy."

Looking over my shoulder, I flipped the loose strands of fly away curls. Placing my big Chanel frames on my face, I rolled my eyes for emphasis. "Yeah I know, I'm riding in my car and you in yours." Getting into my car, I pulled down the overhead mirror puckering my lips. Hassel was cursing me out, he wouldn't dare yell, having the neighbors in our business. Glaring at him, I drove out of our driveway and straight to church. He could either follow suit and catch up or come far behind me looking like the fool he was. Smacking my mouth, I turned on *Won't He Do It* by Koryn Hawthorne. Ready to cause a scene and embarrass my fiancé like he had done me, I prayed about it. I knew it was a big day at church, so I wouldn't risk my father pulling me aside and making me feel his wrath if I mentioned anything.

Pulling into the church parking lot, I spotted most of the members crowded outside. They got on my last nerve. If they weren't congregating to gossip, they were definitely being nosey. Breathing heavily, I put my car in park before opening the door. Spotting my father talking to Hassel's mother, I twisted up my lip in disgust. *How could this woman raise a liar like her son?* I thought, fixing my lips into the fakest smile I could muster.

"Darling where is Hassel?" Henrietta asked, looking over my shoulder for her son that wasn't behind me. Looking over my shoulder for a dramatic effect, I heard Hassel's usual Kirk Franklin playlist in the distance. Shrugging my shoulders, I told her he was right behind me.

"He had to make an extra stop and we didn't want to keep you all waiting." His mother nodded, while my father gave me the stare of death. I'd deal with him later. I figured, there was no escaping him anyway. Walking off, I greeted the church goers before blending into the crowd and into the church.

"Lucy!" I heard Hassel's deep ass voice that once turned me on, yet now it started to annoy me. Turning on my heels, I smirked before waving my finger in his face.

"I don't think you want to bring our premarital problems

into the house of God, now do you?" Placing my hand on my hip, I raised my brow, "I doubt your mother will agree with the fact we live together and we have yet to get married." Knowing exactly what to say to shut him up, he closed his mouth and breathed heavily.

Me and Hassel had been keeping this secret from his mother for two months now. I lived at home with my father until I could no longer take the questions and concerns. My father, Oliver, was one of the top judges in our state and if being his daughter wasn't enough pressure, I fell in love with the pastor's son. Hassel's father passed away last year, resulting in him taking over. It wasn't so bad at first, but hell, as we got closer to our fall wedding date, I started to regret accepting him.

"We're going to talk about this later Lucy." Hassel grabbed my hand, pulling me close to him. Feeling his breath tickle the side of my cheek, my breathing sped up. I knew he wasn't the same guy I had accepted the proposal from and before I got myself mixed-up in his bullshit, I was leaving. My father would kill me if he knew I was dealing with a guy dealing drugs, but if I brought this to his attention without all the proof, I'd lose everything.

Walking hand-in-hand with Hassel, we got on the pulpit as he recited his sermon for the day. Looking off into the crowd, I folded my legs, drifting in and out of thought. Watching my fiancé preach as if he was a child of God, the sweat on his forehead caused me to sift in my seat. I wondered if I was the only one who knew about his street dealings.

Feeling the vibration of my Apple Watch, I saw the name of my best friend flash on the tiny screen. Smiling for the first time today, I looked up and locked eyes with Jen.

Jen: don't look so happy heifer

Pressing the side of the watch, dismissing the green bubble, I fixated back on Hassel as he closed out service.

"And folks, that's what we call a 20/20 vision, amen." I roll my eyes so hard I nearly lost my balance.

"He got some nerve," I mumbled under my breath, standing to my feet. Looking over at my father, I knew he could read the uneasy look on my face. Batting my lashes in his direction, I mouthed *I loved you* before exiting the pulpit.

"Babe, where are you going?"

"I don't feel well Hassel, I'm going to head home. You can stay for afternoon service." Never looking up in his eyes as I spoke, I fidgeted my fingers together.

Lifting my chin with his hand, I stared into his eyes. "I hope this isn't about earlier."

"No, I'm just feeling really uneasy."

"Is your cycle coming?" Hating when he mentioned my period, I smacked my lips.

"Hassel not right now, I'm just not feeling good." Gritting my teeth, it took everything in me not to cause a scene. Stomping off, my heels could be heard across the pavement with much force. Pulling back the doors of the church, I headed straight to my car. My father was calling my name, but the way I was feeling I wasn't trying to hear anything from anyone.

Slamming my door shut, I started the car. Backing out of the parking lot, I headed straight to the house. Holding back the tears that fought to escape, I rubbed my lips together thinking, of the drama that was going to unfold. Once I parked the car, I kicked off my heels at the door and unbuttoned my shirt. Walking through the living room, I unzipped my dress before sliding it down my legs and stepping out of it. Feeling the vibration from my watch, I saw it was Jen calling me for the third time. Dismissing her, I headed straight to the room, grabbing an Armani gray sweat suit to change into. Taking down my bun, I ran my hands through my hair, letting out a sigh. *I was so over this life. I'd hoped by dating someone who wasn't in the streets like Jen or my other homegirls I would get a peaceful life. I* remember thinking I hit the jackpot with Hassel; the preacher's son. My mother was killed due to a senseless act of violence in the streets, so I'd be damned if the same happened to me.

"Yo', that nigga at church, right?" Snapping my neck, I heard the sound of two guys in my house. Creeping over to the walk-in closet in my room. I could hear the voices getting closer. Knowing that my closet had a slight squeak to it, I waited until one of them began talking again before drawing it back swiftly. Feeling my heartbeat sped up and the queasy feeling in my stomach, I swallowed hard, sliding behind the dresses lined up.

"I know that nigga got them bricks in this house, he ain't that smart to not have it here." The voice sounded familiar, yet I couldn't depict who it belonged to. Trying not to breathe heavily, the beads of sweat formed on my forehead and around my top lip. *I'm going to kill this nigga! I swear,* I thought, shaking my head back and forth. Hearing the door hit the wall with force from them storming in, I heard the sound of a car in the driveway. Praying to God it was Hassel or my father, I let the tears fall down my cheek. Licking my lips, I taste the salty tears that rested there. Holding in my cries, Hassel could be heard shouting in the distance. I wanted to warn him about the guys in the house, but I knew they were strapped. Peeking from behind one of the dresses, I looked through the crack in the closet.

"Shit," I mumbled when I saw one of them standing by the doorway with his gun drawn.

"Nah, I told them dudes don't fuck with me! They got the right nigga today!" Hassel must have been on a call because I couldn't hear anyone else talking. Using this as my opportunity, I went to my watch, pulling up my call log I tapped his number.

"Fuck this bitch want? Yo Iman, let me call you back yo." Chuckling to myself and shaking my head, I ended the call just as gunfire erupted. At the sound of multiple gunshots going off, I ducked far into the closet; hiding.

"God if I survive this, I swear I'll never mess with another fuck boy again. Sorry, I mean a liar." When the gunfire came to a stop, I hesitated to come out. "Lucy, Lucy you good?" When he shouted for me, I nearly jumped out of my skin. "Lucy, if you in here, call for help! Them niggas is dead!"

Jumping out from the closet, I saw the first guy laid out by the bedroom door. Stepping over him, I saw Hassel up against the wall with a gunshot to his stomach. "What the fuck Hassel?"

"Bitch, just call for help!" Never hearing him call me out my name, I sucked my teeth.

"Fuck you, Hassel!" Looking over my shoulder, I saw the other guy on the floor in a pool of blood. Stepping over Hassel, he reached for my pants leg. Kicking at him, I told him he better call for his own help.

"You disrespected me for the last time, oh and you're the bitch, pussy." Taking the stairs two at a time, I grabbed my car keys and purse with my phone inside. Hopping in my car, I sped off after dialing Jen's number.

"Girl, why the hell you ain't answer my call?" Jen yelled into the receiver, displaying her attitude.

"Listen Jen, I can't even get into that right now, all I'ma say is I'm going to go stay at my cousin Misha's house in New York for a little." Jumping on the highway, I placed my gear on cruise control for the rest of the drive.

"New York, what the fuck Lou?"

"I'll explain once I get to her house."

"Nah heifer, explain right fucking now!" Hearing commotion in the background, I overheard someone mention Hassel's name. "Lou, did you know that Hassel got shot?" Jen continued, asking me over and over as I got my thoughts together, blocking her frantic voice.

"Dammit Jen! Yes, I know he got shot. He's been in the streets, and them niggas came busting off shots in his house." Tapping the steering wheel in frustration, I ended up in traffic on I-95.

"You're not making any sense Lou, were you involved in the shooting?" Snapping my neck, I pressed the red phone on my iPhone 11, ending the call.

Jen had crossed the line asking me if I was involved when she knew how hard I fought to stay clear of that life. I had known Jen all my life, so she was aware of my mother's death as a child. Grabbing my phone, I put it on do not disturb for the rest of the drive.

****TEN HOURS LATER ****

Welcome to New York, the sign read, causing me to let out a loud sigh. Only stopping once, I was drained and needed a shower. Stopping at a gas station, I needed to stretch my legs. Slamming the door shut, I scrolled down my notifications on my home screen. Between the calls from my father and Jen, I noticed the text from Hassel asking if I was okay, to him calling me all types of bitches and hoes. He wouldn't know if I was hoe cuz the nigga never felt my pussy. I wasn't a virgin, but I was following our vows and waiting to our wedding day. Glad I did, thinking about it now. Entering the store, I grabbed a few snacks before I sent a text to my cousin, letting her know I was less than an hour away. Paying for the items, I noticed it was almost eight at night and I hadn't had a meal yet.

Running back to my car, I hopped in my black 2019 BMW sucking my teeth at yet another disrespectful text from Hassel. Starting up the engine, I turned on the latest song I'd been hooked to, *Heart on My Ice* by Rod Wave. Bopping my head to the words, pointing my index finger in the mirror singing along, *"It's my fault, I wear my heart on my sleeve."* Biting my bottom lip, I backed out just as a car brushed up alongside of my bumper.

The fuck! I thought, whipping my head around to see a black Range Rover skidding up the block before coming to a complete stop. Grabbing the gear, I placed my car in park. Opening the middle console, I pulled the blade out, tucking it in my hand. "This nigga better explain what the fuck just happened and quick," I mumble on the way to the car that had come to a complete stop. A dude stepped out from the driver's side rubbing his hand across his head. *Damn he was fine!*

Shaking off the feeling, I shouted walking in his direction. "You ain't see me fucking backing out from the gas station?" I shouted with my heavy southern accent. Ignoring what he was saying, I released my blade, "I should cut your stupid ass right now yo!" The dude jumped back just in time, causing me to miss his chest by an inch.

"Bitch is you crazy?" Side eyeing me, he grabbed my wrist, pulling me towards him. Before I could protest and fight him off, he began laughing hysterically. Furrowing my brows, I shouted obscene words at him before pulling back from him and walking back to my car.

"Yeah, take that little ass back in the car."

Flipping him the middle finger, I hopped in my driver's seat. Backing out yet again, he stood off to the side with a cocky smirk on his face. Shaking my head in annoyance, he told me he would see me again. Racing down the highway, I drove straight to Misha's house with my adrenaline on a hundred.

2

HASSEL

"This bitch has lost her fucking marbles!" Leaning up against the wall in the house, I scanned the hallway where the dude was laying covered in blood. Unable to get up as fast as I wanted, I overheard a gurgling sound on the other end. Praying this dude was near death; I didn't have the strength to finish him off. Pulling myself up, I gripped my side.

"I really can't believe this shit," mumbling to myself, I poked my head out, glaring at the dude gripping his neck for dear life. Limping towards the stairs, I heard the sirens in the distance, with my phone in one hand, the other holding my side, I dragged myself down the steps. Feeling the vibration in my hand, I saw Oliver calling me. Allowing it to go to voicemail and sliding down the last step, a police officer met me.

"Put your hands up!"

"I live here, I'm shot nigga!" I responded through clenched teeth.

"I said put your hands up!" Reaching to his side to draw his gun back, my mother shouted my name.

"Officer, he's the pastor! This is his house!" she cried out.

Becoming lightheaded, I stretched out my free arm to hold onto the bannister. Falling over, I passed out.

WAKING up in the hospital surrounded by family and the police, I sucked my teeth. The look on my mother's face displayed disgust. Now I had to explain shit to her that I wasn't ready for. Scanning all the people in the room, there was no sign of Lucy. Easing up in the bed, I felt the restraints from the handcuffs on my right arm. Forcibly moving my arm back and forth, the officers told me to relax.

"We have plenty of questions for you, relax and hopefully these will be removed." Throwing my body back onto the hospital bed, my stomach clenched up in pain from the wound. Clearing out the room, the two officers took my statement.

"So, where is your fiancée? She had nothing to do with this?"

"Fuck that bitch, she left me for dead!" Squinting my eyes with anger, my breathing sped up.

"We're going to need her name and her license plate."

"Shouldn't be too hard to find her, she's the daughter of Oliver Hinton."

The officer closed the notepad, Walking towards me, he questioned if I was sure.

"Nigga, I know who I was marrying, so go ask him where his daughter Lucy is." Looking over at the next officer who wasn't the least bit amused, I asked, "Can these come off my arm?"

"Explain the cocaine that was found in the house."

"Now I know you know who my fiancée's mother was; c'mon now, that shit runs in the family," I reply, dismissing the allegations of any of the drugs in the house being mine. I knew Lucy's mother's secret; using this shit to my advantage right now would hopefully work. I was a preacher; I had no time to go to jail. Shit, it was only one brick in the crib anyway, I could work that off and still deal with my connect.

The officer with the notepad nodded, removed the handcuffs and turned on his heels to walk away. The second officer gave me one more glance before following suit.

"I'll be damned if this selfish bitch gets off easy," I murmured as my mother came rushing in behind them.

"Now tell me, what in the devil happened in that house?" My mother pulled up an empty chair close by. "They said one of the guys was already dead and the other fighting for his life."

Nearly losing my breath, I looked over at my mother, "Were there any updates?"

"No, but we need to go pray for him. I already know it was that fast tail girl that got you caught up in this." Punching my arm playfully, she continued, "And I found out she's been living with you." Shaking her head and folding her arms, she leaned back in the chair.

"Yeah ma, she ain't no good, and I messed up." Rubbing my tongue over my teeth, I wanted to drop the subject before more shit came out.

"Well I'ma let you rest. Don't go trying to reach out to that little hussy either."

Nodding in her direction, as soon as she walked out the room, I scanned it for my phone. Coming across it in the chair, I slid out of the bed. Looking at the missed calls and texts, I noticed one from Jen.

Jen- I don't know what you did to my girl, but trust, this will not be the end of it Hass.

Dialing up Lucy's number, the phone went straight to voicemail. I was fucked up for throwing her in the mix, but shit, I needed the heat taken off of me until I could figure out a plan. Shooting her a text, I prayed she read it before the cops caught up to her or her father.

3

ASAAD

atching shorty drive off, I had to catch myself from laughing again. She really tried to fucking cut me over brushing up against her. Rubbing my teeth over my gums, my cell phone rang, pulling me back from my daydream. Looking down the phone, Gabby's name flashed with a corny heart emoji next to it. Shaking my head, I mumbled to myself, "This bitch is getting on my last nerve touching my fucking phone."

"Yo!" Obviously agitated with her high pitched voice, her dumbass didn't even catch the attitude I threw her way.

"Baby, I was wondering when you were coming back this way."

Rolling my eyes, I replied, "Gabby, I won't be there for a minute, I gotta go stop at the buildings and check on my fucking tenants," cursing her out, knowing she wouldn't give a damn.

"Aight, fine, Assad." Gabby must have been pouting them big ass lips that I loved wrapped around my dick.

"Just be up when I get in the damn house Gabby, I mean ass

naked and the only time you should be using your mouth is to wrap it around my dick!"

"I got you, Zaddy," she purred into the phone, which turned me off.

Gabby was my wife; I wouldn't say wife for long cuz me and her were in the midst of a divorce. We outgrew each other, but she still wanted to feel, suck and fuck from time to time. Who was I to deny her that shit? We still lived in the house we purchased two years ago. She was on one end I was on the other. The only time we ran into each other was when she wanted some dick or some spending money.

The living arrangement was crazy, but shit, we got used to it. We both needed the money and wanted a divorce. Turning into the block where one of my properties were, I dialed up Chinx, my right hand man.

"What's the word?"

"Listen, I know we were supposed to link up, but I got side-tracked at the gas station." Rubbing my hand across the top of my head, I looked out my side view mirror just as two of the tenants were arguing with each other. Shaking my head in disgust, I turned my attention back to my boy on the line.

"Yeah aight, nigga it's Friday. You know Gabby trying to suck ya ass dry, so you won't wake up." Chuckling into the line, I told him to shut the fuck up.

"Nigga don't make me call Dazzle on your ass," I warned him, mentioning his baby mama who still had a hold on the nigga.

"Fuck you, but for real, I gotta go check on these apartments," Chinx responded laughing.

"Yeah, first of the month, I know how that go."

Ending the call with Chinx, I stepped out of the car, walking up on the two tenants who were still arguing.

"Y'all not serious, right? Both of y'all's kids are out here looking like shit, it's late, and y'all arguing?" The woman with the loudest mouth turned to face me with her hands on her wide hips.

"This bitch keep leaving her water on flooding my apartment, Asaad!"

"Bitch you just mad cuz ya baby daddy been upstairs kicking it with me while you at your WEP program." Holding in her laughter, I twisted up my lips in their direction.

"Y'all bitches arguing over a bum-ass nigga like Charlie?" Frustrated with the both of them, I shook my head walking off, leaving them to continue arguing. Jogging up to the management office, I spotted Halimah, my assistant.

"Hey Asaad, two tenants were short on rent this month." Looking down at the time, I asked her what she was doing here this late while she slid me a paper.

"Which two?" I asked, not really wanting an answer, because I already figured which two it was.

"Misha and Erica, and to answer your other question, I'm here because I needed to get out of my house for a breather," she stated, not looking up from her notebook.

Taken aback when she mentioned Misha's name, I replied, "Nah, something gotta be wrong for Misha to be short." Huffing, I ran my hand through my thick beard. Paying her a visit, I banged on her apartment door. Hearing yelling on the other end, I pounded harder on the door.

"Who is it?"

"Asaad." Hearing the locks click over, I stood back a little. Coming face-to-face with the chick from the gas station.

"Oh, hell no. Misha, you know this rude muthafucka?" She snaked her neck around to face Misha, who was obviously taller than her.

Misha shrugged her off. "He's my landlord Lou, how you know him?"

Licking her pink, plump lips, she squinted her almond-shaped eyes in my direction. "He's the dude I told you who tried to kill me earlier!" Shaking her head and popping her mouth for emphasis, I laughed at her.

"Misha, I ain't try to kill ol' girl, sis the one who tried to shank a nigga." Letting myself into the two-bedroom apartment, I closed the door behind me. "I need to talk to you about the rent."

"Yeah, I know I'm short Asaad. I promise I'll have it before the weekend is up." Lou snapped her neck and folded her arms across her small chest.

"How short is she?"

Giving Misha a knowing look, Lou jumped in front of me waving her arms. "How short?" Grabbing a small purse she pulled out a small wad of cash.

"Three hundred." Peeling off the fifties, she handed me the cash.

"That should be all of it. Thanks, you can go now." Using her small hand, she pushed on my chest.

"Listen you good, I'ma bounce, but Misha I still want to talk to you." Turning on my heels, I walked out just as Lou slammed the door shut in my face. "Bitch," I mumbled to no one in particular.

Leaving out the apartment complex, I headed straight to my house, praying Gabby was sleeping. Pulling into the driveway, I noticed the kitchen light on as well as the living room light. Knowing it meant Gabby was wide awake fucked up my whole mood. Looking over my shoulder, I turned around shaking my head. Reaching over into my middle console, I pulled out a half smoked blunt. Lighting it up, I rolled down the window a little before taking my first pull. Using the lever on the side of the driver's seat, I adjust it to recline back. Lifting the small lit blunt wrapped in backwoods paper to my lips, I choked back my cough. Exhaling the gray smoke and slowly inhaling it in my nostrils, I heard tapping on the window. With the effect of the weed mixed with the stress I was feeling, I nearly dropped the blunt on my leg. Looking at Gabby like she was a mad woman through glazed eyes, I roll the window all the way down. Her hair was disheveled and every time she shouted; her neck snapped for emphasis. Gabby yelled a bunch of bullshit I wasn't trying to hear. Smelling the liquor on her breath explained her outburst. Unlocking the door, I placed my hand on the lever, pulling it in my direction and popping the door open. She jumped back. Clasping her wool robe together, she held on as the night air ripped through it.

"Are you fucking crazy Gabby?" Not waiting on an answer, I told her to take her ass back in the house.

"Asaad I'm in the house waiting on you and you're out here smoking. What type of shit is that?"

"Gabby, I don't give a damn what type of shit it is to you, get the fuck in the house and leave me alone."

Fed up with her bullshit, I hopped back in the car and backed out the driveway.

$$4$$

LOU

*"Just when you think you're getting peace of mind, the bullshit
begins."*

My cell phone was ringing back-to-back for the past hour with calls from my father, Jen, and Hassel. Asking Misha where her liquor cabinet was, she told me she didn't have any more at home. Giving her the stare of death, I asked her was she pregnant again or something. Misha was my party cousin, so for her not to have any liquor in the house only meant she was knocked up with her third child from her useless ass baby father.

"I'm not pregnant Lou, I'm just broke!" She sounded depressed, too damn depressed if you ask me.

"How much money do you need Misha?"

"I'm not taking your money girl; you already got enough shit going on."

Shrugging her off, I told her I was stepping out. I didn't tell her the full rundown on what happened as far as the shooting.

I wasn't trying to scare her off from allowing me to stay here and I wasn't trying to book none of these expensive ass hotels.

Getting into my car, I pulled out my phone and saw a message from Hassel.

Hubby: listen Lucy, it's a lot of shit going on down here, you're gonna have to talk to the police

Twisting up my lip, him mentioning the police gave me a sour taste in my mouth. I didn't do anything but leave him before I got my name mixed up in anything, and here it was, my name was mixed up in bullshit anyway. Calling up my father, he was beyond pissed.

"Lou, the next time you decide to skip town after you witness some bullshit, you let me know little girl!" he chastised me as if I was a child instead of a twenty-seven year old woman.

Sucking my teeth before speaking, I replied "Dad, I left because Hassel was dealing drugs and I knew I couldn't bring it to you without proof." Catching my breath before speaking again, I said, "I know how you are about these things and then when the shooting—"

Cutting me off, my father told me don't talk any more over the phone. Letting him know I was at Misha's house, he told me to book a hotel and to stay away from her apartment. My father was overprotective and he didn't approve of the fact that I was with my cousin from my mother's side who turned tricks.

"Dad, you act like I'm about to be out here selling my pussy. I'm not doing anything but laying low!"

"Lucy, I said what the fuck I said. I'll be up there first thing tomorrow." Ending the call, I banged my fist on the steering wheel in a fit. Starting up the car, I drove until I found a bar nearby. Wanting to go search for a hotel, I knew my father would be pissed if he found out I went back to Misha's. Parking the car, I headed in, taking a seat closest to the door.

My hair that was once pulled up in a messy bun, was now hanging down my shoulders. My sweat suit was wrinkled from sitting all day. Applying a coat of clear lip gloss from Mac to my lips, I flagged down the bartender.

"How can I help you?" He looked to be about twenty-three, could have been younger, who knows?

"Yeah, I'ma take a double shot of Hennessy, please." Furrowing his brows, he looked back at me and asked was I sure.

I wanted to curse him out for asking such a stupid question, but instead I nodded. Pulling out my phone again as it vibrated, Jen sent a text telling me the cops asked her was I into illegal dealings. Huffing, I knew it had to be Hassel lying on me. His mother would kill him before a gang member did if she knew he was running the streets.

The bartender returned with the drink. Lifting the glass and throwing back the shot, it burned my chest. Letting out a slight gasp and sticking out my tongue, I reached inside my purse.

"It's already paid for." Following his eyes, I looked right into the eyes of Asaad. Dipping my head to the side, I smiled inwardly. Making his way over to the empty barstool beside me, his hand brushed down my back.

"Why you in this bar so late? Better yet, why are you alone?"

Swiveling on the stool, I turned to face him. The effect of the drink mixed with my exhaustion caused my eyelids to hang low. "You're not my father. I'm a grown ass woman and I'm here visiting my cousin who you know can't get out much."

Biting down on his bottom lip, Asaad side eyed me before answering. "You got a smart ass mouth for a chick who's clearly from out of state. I'ma let it slide because you don't know any better, but that shit ain't gonna work on all New York niggas."

"I don't care what works for what niggas; I ain't here for y'all." Turning the seat away from him, I waved down the bartender again.

"Another round," I said, whirling my finger in the air, letting him know to give me what I just had. Shit I was pissed off, stressed out and now horny thanks to Assad's fine, cocky ass. Getting up and standing behind me, Asaad bent down. The hair on the back of my neck stood at attention. Closing my legs tightly together and biting my bottom lip, I stared straight ahead. My gaze in the mirror met Asaad's.

"What you jumping for me? You scared of me?"

Licking my bottom lip, I replied, "No, but I don't like niggas this close to me." Leaning forward into my ear he whispered that he wasn't just any nigga; he was *that* nigga.

Shit. I squeezed my pussy muscles tight, stopping the fire that burned between my legs. My pussy throbbed. *This nigga got me fucked up*, I thought. *How the hell he got my pussy this wet with just a few words?*

I blame this shit on Hassel. Had he been handling his business as a man and not being a fake pastor, I wouldn't be on this drought. I couldn't even remember the last time I felt dick. I'd been masturbating for so long that I didn't care about dick. I thought I didn't care, but the way I was leaking right now and the way my nipples grew under my sweatshirt from arousal, I cared.

"Assad, move boy." Swaying my head to the side, he laughed before sitting down again.

"So, what's your story country girl?"

"My name is Lou and I don't have a story. What about you landlord?"

"Well shit, I thought y'all people were fucking friendly."

"I'm not people, I'm Lou!"

"You got that, but ain't shit. I'm a landlord getting my money."

"You're also married." Smacking my lips, I glared at the black wedding band that was covered in diamonds.

"Your ass ain't slick, I see the incoming text reading hubby on ya line, so that's just a nigga hitting you off, huh?"

"I'm not married, but we ain't talking about me, we talking about you."

"Hmm," he replied, rubbing his hand over his face. The wrinkles in his forehead let me know he was thinking hard about what to say.

"So what's your story?" Folding my legs on top of each other, I stared into his cold eyes. Watching him throw back another shot of cognac, he swallowed the brown liquor with ease.

"It ain't nothing you gotta worry about miss, you smoke?" he asked fixing his gray sweats he wore. Noticing the bulge in his pants, I quickly looked away. "What you looking at it for? You can't handle this country."

Wanting to prove his cocky ass wrong, I decided against it. Twisting up my lips, I looked away just as my phone showed another text from Hassel. Rolling my eyes, I took the phone in my hand, excused myself and walked to the back of the bar, annoyed. Dialing his number, I waited for him to answer.

"Lucy, where the hell are you?" As always, his arrogance annoyed me.

"That's none of ya concern, why are you blowing me up Hassel?" Leaning up against the wall, I used my free hand to toss the loose strands of curls out of my face. Hot and bothered, I heard him rambling on and on about the events earlier. My attention was fixated on Asaad, with his eyes low, he took a pull from the blunt.

"Do you hear me Lucy?" he asked, snapping out of the trance Asaad had me in. Shit, this was a whole married man; I'm bugging.

"What?" I replied, obviously pissed with him bringing me back to reality.

"I said when you coming home?" Pulling the phone away from me, I looked at it with a screw face.

"You asked, you didn't say and I'm not, so lose my number

bitch!" Ending the call before he could annoy me further, I tuck my iPhone in my purse. Entering the bathroom and walking to the sink, I cut on the water. Splashing it on my face, I was losing my mind. Lusting over this married nigga and hiding from my ex fiancé. Hearing the door squeak, the music became louder. Rubbing my hands across my face fast, I wasn't about to get caught slipping in New York by none of these grimy hoes.

Being forced to turn around and pinned to the wall, I know he could see the fright on my face. "Relax country." Lifting my hands above my head with one of his hands, Asaad used his free hand to slip it down the front of my sweats.

"Shit," I mumbled just as his finger brushed across the thin material of my thong. I was hoping he didn't hear me but the cocky smile on his face told me different. Lowering his head to mine, he hungrily kissed my mouth. Using his tongue, he pried my mouth open. Unable to move my hands, I squirmed from his touch. Dipping his finger in between my folds, I let out a moan in his mouth.

Asaad used his leg to spread mine open, dipping a finger inside of me. I ground on him. Closing my eyes I told myself, *think about anything bitch! You better not come!* Thinking about anything but how good his finger felt inside of me, my body jolted forward with each thrust.

"Ahh, I'm going to cum," I whined into his ear.

"Do that shit then." I needed this nigga to say don't cum yet, instead, he encouraged this cream pie that was long overdue. On cue, my body froze as Asaad's finger massaged my g spot. I came all over him.

Releasing my arms and laying my head back on the wall, he removed his hand from my sweats. Taking his finger in his mouth, he sucked my juices from it. Looking down at his manhood, it stood straight up. "Don't worry 'bout this, you ain't ready for him yet." Cocking my head to the side, I chuckled.

"Says who?"

"As hard as you came and as tight as you were, I'm sure it's been awhile."

"Whatever, you wasn't about to feel this pussy anyway." Lying more to myself than him, I stepped around him. The sticky substance on my thong pissed me off. I now needed a shower and a good night's sleep.

"Yea aight, I'll see ya little ass around." Watching him walk out of the bathroom, I wanted to tell him to come put it on me, but shit, I was in a public restroom. Against my father's wishes, I ended up right back at Misha's door.

5

MISHA

The banging on my front door had just woke me from my slumber. Really needing the sleep, I prayed whoever it was had a damn good excuse. Reaching over on my queen-sized bed, my phone read two in the morning. Rolling my eyes, I slid out of bed before the visitor woke up my kids. Stumbling out the room, kicking over toys in the hallway, I shouted for them to stop knocking. Wiping the sleep from my eyes, I looked through the peephole. Sucking my teeth, I saw Lou on the other end dancing from side to side.

Pulling back the door, I grabbed her ass in the house. "Bitch, I could kill you, banging like the fucking police."

"Sorry." Lowering her head, I could smell the liquor on her breath. Brushing past me, she headed in the direction of the bathroom.

"Where the hell were you?" Knowing Oliver couldn't stand Lou around me, I sure didn't need her getting into any trouble up here.

"I was out," she said through a sigh as she relieved herself. "You know I'm grown, right Misha?"

"I don't give a fuck; Oliver will not be knocking on my door questioning me about any bullshit you got yourself caught up in." Sitting down on my sofa, I grabbed the remote cutting on the television.

"Can you give me a towel and shit? I need a shower." Shaking my head, I hopped up from the couch. Lou knew where I kept the damn towels, this wasn't her first time here, nor did I live in a lavish house like hers. I stayed in a rundown tenement building in the Bronx on 167 and Sheridan. Sure wasn't one of them upscale newly renovated places, but it also wasn't the pissy projects.

Walking down the small hallway, I rummaged through the closet in search of a towel without bleach stains. Hearing my phone ring in my bedroom I sighed, it could only be one person at this hour and I wasn't in the mood for his bullshit. Pulling out a dark maroon colored towel and washcloth, I opened the bathroom and tossed them on the sink. Stepping into my room, I picked up my Samsung phone. Don had called and texted me five times. He was probably tipsy and wanted to come crash or to get some pussy. Flopping down on the bed, the mattress shifted a little from my weight. Against my better judgement, I hit the call button and waited to hear his deep baritone voice.

"What the fuck ya fat ass doing?" Groaning into the line, I wasn't sure why I had made the call.

"It's two in the morning Don, I was sleeping."

"You sure you was sleeping and not choking on the next nigga dick?"

I was pissed off that every chance he got he would throw up my profession in my face. Don knew I turned tricks, shit that's how I met him ten years ago. Placing my head in my hand, I counted to ten before giving him my attention.

"Don don't call my phone on no bullshit. What is it you want?"

"To come get my dick wet, the fuck else?" Taping my foot

impatiently on the black and white tiled floor, I thought about Lou being here. Although I'd never turn down Don, I knew if Lou saw him coming over, she would get in my ass. Go figure, I was older than her by a few years, yet she was the one who was hostile and bossy.

"Don, I'll come to you."

"The fuck you talking about? Nah, I'm coming over. I'll be there in five minutes." Before I could protest, the sound of the call ending pissed me off. Jumping up from the bed, I searched my room for the easiest outfit I could get on. I wasn't about to try and squeeze into some jeans, I was a healthy size 12 with hips and ass for days. Settling in on some gray leggings and a T-shirt, I pulled them up my leg. The sound of the knocker made my heart speed up.

"Who the hell is it?" I heard Lou shout as her flip flops slapped across the floor.

"Shit," I murmured, jogging out of my room and into the living room. Don was standing in the living room with a look of lust plastered on his face, while Lou had her lips turned up at him. Standing with a towel wrapped around her petite body and her naturally curly hair dripping wet, I asked her to go in the room. Turning on her heels, she shook her head and mumbled to me that I better be careful messing with him. Little did she know he was the father of my oldest child and possibly father to my youngest.

"Who the fuck was that?" Pointing his finger down the hallway, he reeked of Tequila.

"None of ya business. I told you let me come to you but you was against it."

"Cuz I don't want your ass around my niggas, how many times I gotta tell your fat ass that?" Feeling my stomach go queasy, I prayed Lou wasn't listening to Don degrade me. Apparently, I was good enough to fuck behind closed doors but not be seen with in public. Shit, I wasn't always this thick, and yes thick, cuz I'm far from sloppy.

After my second son, I had put on more weight than I anticipated and the lack of happiness caused me to pile it on faster. Standing with my hands on my hips, I bit on my bottom lip while Don told me how my weight needed to be handled. When he met me, I was a size eight, every chance he got he made it known.

"Misha, I know you're not letting this drunk muthafucka talk down on you like you ain't that bitch!" My eyes widened in fright when I turned to face Lou.

"Nigga, get ya bum-ass up out of here with that shit. My cousin is a bad bitch, and before I let her fuck ya limp dick ass I'ma kick you out." Brushing past me, she pushed him on his chest towards the door. Don was too drunk to keep his balance, stumbling backward.

"Bitch have you lost ya mind?" Don shouted at Lou who ignored him.

"You got two minutes to get ya funky ass outta here before you meet my blade nigga!" Don hopped up so fast from the floor, leaving out the apartment. He told me he was going to fuck me up next time he saw me.

Before I could close the door fully, Lou was standing there shaking her head and waving her finger in my face.

"I can't believe you Misha, you always the one quick to tell me about myself, yet you letting that bum-ass drunk walk over you!"

"Before you go off on me Lou, let me explain this shit to you."

"Nah, you good sis, you let that nigga call you fat and you're far from it." Glaring in my direction, I felt her eyes burning a hole in me. "He probably ain't got enough dick to get past ya ass, that's why he's complaining." No longer able to hold in my laughter I shook my head at Lou.

"Alright, I get it. Listen, I'm tired and I'm sure you're tired too." Looking at the bags under her eyes, she nodded at me.

"You damn right, and tomorrow we are going shopping, so get enough sleep." Lou had a sheet and a pillow in her arms as she flopped on the couch. Stretching out, I headed straight to my room where my message notification was lit up. Too tired to entertain it, I pulled down my knotless dark brown and blonde braids from the high ponytail. Slipping out of the leggings and pulling the shirt over my head, I laid across my bed. Too tired to remove the eyebrow pencil I wore on a daily basis; I buried my head into the pillow before passing out.

6

LOU

"NOW I KNOW SHIT JUST GOT REAL!"

For the first time in the past 24-hours, I had some of the best sleep. Probably was due to the nut I had earlier or the fact I wasn't laid up under Hassel's stinking breath ass. Rolling over slightly, I fell right off the small sofa landing on the hardwood floors. Forgetting I was in Misha's house, I heard the snickering from her two sons. Peeking my eyes open, they sat at the dining room table looking over their shoulders. Groaning, I pulled myself up from the floor just as the banging on Misha's door began again.

"This is the second time, what the fuck is going on in this damn house?" Wrapping the top sheet around my exposed bottom, I peeped through the peephole only growing more annoyed. Pulling the door back, my father barged his way in without an invite.

"I could have sworn I told your ass to get a fucking hotel, Lucy!" The ruckus must have woken Misha up because she appeared in the living room with a scowl on her face. I never knew what their beef was, but I knew that whatever happened with them was far from over. Looking past me, his eyes landed on Misha, yanking me by my arm. "Go get your shit on right now little girl, don't make me repeat myself!" The outspoken, blade wielding woman I was yesterday was long gone. I knew better than to play with Oliver when he spoke.

His six foot frame and masculine voice intimidated me on impulse. Never wanting to question his judgment, I looked over at Misha who folded her arms across her chest, raising her brow.

"She's not going anywhere, Oliver."

"Bitch, I'm not talking to you, worry about them damn kids of your own and less about my child." Turning away from her, he said, "I said get ya shit Lucy Hinton!" Swallowing hard, I left to grab my sweat suit, throwing it on and handling my hygiene.

The bickering between the two of them was starting to annoy me and I'm sure the kids wanted to know what the beef was. Leaving out of the bathroom, my curly hair was all over my head.

"I'm ready." Hanging my head low, I followed behind him to where our cars were parked.

"You out here running behind that whore and your ass is wanted for fucking drugs in North Carolina!" My father shouted so loud I thought one of the neighbors would call the police. Walking up in my personal space, he bent down to my level. "If I find out you out here acting fucking stupid Lucy, I'm going to lock your ass up myself." Biting on my bottom lip to stop it from trembling, the tears welled in my eyes. With each threat my father spewed, I looked around at the onlookers who were being nosey. Talk about fucking embarrassing; I wasn't a little girl, yet at this moment, I felt like I was a teenager.

"I hear you daddy," I replied, just above a whisper.

"Now, go get in that car and follow behind me, do you hear me?" Nodding at him, I followed behind him to where my BMW was parked. Hearing someone call my name, I whipped my head around to the familiar voice. It was Asaad. Walking in my direction, he looked good as fuck and I still had on the sweat suit from the day before. Looking over at my father, who gave me a knowing glare, I ignored Asaad and got in the car. Starting up the engine, I pulled off before he could reach my car.

"Fuck!" hitting my steering wheel in frustration, I tailed behind my father until he pulled into a hotel parking lot. Plugging my phone up to my charger, I realized it was dead. I knew Misha had sent me numerous texts.

My father walked up to my car, tapping on the window. I rolled it down. "Yeah?"

"I brought you a bag of clothes, we are going to go up there and change while you tell me what the fuck happened in that house."

"Dad, I don't know what happened in that house!" Raising my voice at him, he reached in popping me in my mouth. Letting out a slight whimper, I held onto my busted lip.

"Keep playing with me Lucy, you're going to make me rip you a new asshole!"

Rolling up my window, I got out the car without saying another word. Trailing behind him, I used my sweatshirt to hold my bloodied lip. Once we were in the room, I took the bag from him and went in the bathroom. Looking in the mirror, I allowed the tears to fall. My father could be a mean bastard when he wanted but also a sweetheart if I followed all his rules to a T. Taking a washcloth, I cleaned my face, opening the overnight bag he packed. It held my makeup case along with a pair of jeans, a hoodie and a pair of my Jordans. Hopping in the shower, I let my phone charge, so I could text Misha and let her know I was good.

Twenty minutes later, I was all cried out and shriveled up, hoping I could stay in the bathroom forever. I knew it was only a matter of time before my father would start banging on the door. Stepping out of the shower, I grabbed the white towel drying my body off. I found my coconut oil stashed in the corner of the bag. Oiling my body, the vibration of my phone caught my attention.

Misha: Girl, what is your father's problem?

Misha: Hello?

Misha: little girl, I know you better answer me and fast

Looking towards the door before responding to Misha, I told her I was fine and I'd call her as soon as I got in my car away from my father. She replied with a dry *okay.*

Pulling the jeans up my legs and throwing the hoodie over my head, I applied the concealer, foundation and pink lip gloss to my bruised lips. Hoping to disguise the slight cut, I grabbed my Chanel frames and exited the bathroom.

"Bout damn time. I know you were avoiding me, but Lucy I don't give a fuck." Looking at him through the dark shades, I rolled my eyes before flopping down on the king-sized bed.

"This shit ain't no joke and they're trying to charge you for that brick they found at y'all's house." Snapping my neck back, I removed the frames from my face.

"Daddy, you know that shit ain't mine. Hassel has been supplying the fucking neighborhood for some time and I got proof."

Sitting in the reclining chair, I stared at my father's foot tap against the floor impatiently. His jaw clenched as he cracked his knuckles.

"What proof Lou?" The only time he called me Lou was when he needed shit taken care of. Fumbling with my phone and unlocking it, I searched through it until I came across the picture of the brick along with a list. Hassel didn't know I had snapped a picture of the list under the brick. I wasn't green to the street shit. My mother was a queen pin up here in New York City and every chance she got she would give me information on how shit was ran while my father went to work.

My father snatched my phone from my hand, looking at the

labeling on the package, he spotted something on the paper that caught his attention.

"Send me a copy of this shit Lou and right now!"

With my nerves on a hundred, I did what I was told, Daddy, umm I have a voice clip from Hassel."

Whirling his finger, he told me to play it for him. The look of disgust on my father's face when he heard Hassel ask how I thought we could afford the shit we had.

"When were you going to bring me this shit, Lou!" My father banged his hand on the chair. Jumping back, my heart pounded as my breathing sped up.

"I was trying to wait until I could get more information, daddy."

My father's green eyes turned cold; the dimples that usually adorned his face were hidden. His caramel complexion was now red. "Stay your ass right here, I'm going to handle something." Jumping up, he turned back in my direction. With a menacing look, he added, "If I find out you left here Lucy, I'm going to snap them twig legs of yours."

"I understand." Hoping he hurried up and left out of my face, I quickly dialed Misha.

"Girl, I need you to ask ya mom to keep the kids and hurry up and get to this hotel room."

"Okay, but what's the emergency?" Misha got on my nerves asking questions over the phone all the time instead of listening to me.

"I can't say, oh and where did Asaad go?"

"I guess out with his wife, I saw him with some flowers in his car." Rolling my eyes, I became jealous as I bit my lip. He wasn't my man and he was married, so who did I think I was?

"Oh aight, well just hurry up." Ending the call, I sat back on the bed scrolling through my Facebook and Instagram. Going to my direct messages, I saw Jen had sent me a few memes.

Scrolling to her name, I FaceTimed her, "Bitch what the fuck?"

"Jen, I don't know what Hassel is telling people, but apparently he trying to pin shit on me."

"Yeah, I know that cuz it's all down here in Raleigh."

"Well I didn't do any of that stuff."

"Girl please, I know. Your little country ass try to act hard but you're not at all."

Chuckling at her statement, she was definitely right. My father raised me to stand up for myself if I had too but I wasn't into any drama. With my mother having a record, I was told if I ever fucked with the law, Oliver would put his foot up my ass. I wasn't scared of much, but of him, I was petrified. He didn't beat me growing up but one time and I told myself that night I would never cross the line again.

"Anyway, are you good?"

"Yeah, I'm good. I mean, I had some nigga make me nut girl."

"Girl, I know you ain't fuck somebody that damn quick?"

"Technically no but—" the light tapping on the door stopped me mid-sentence. "Jen, let me call you back." Not waiting on a response, I sprinted over to the door. Looking through the small peephole I saw Misha standing there. Pulling open the door, she dropped her head in my direction.

"Now, explain what's going on and where is your father?"

"He left for a few."

7

HASSEL

Sitting up in the hospital bed, my phone hasn't stopped ringing since I woke up yesterday. Feeling a migraine coming on, I placed my hand on my temples, pressing lightly. I closed my eyes. Unable to get in touch with Lucy, I was starting to see she was definitely dodging me. When word got out that my house was broken into, my plug eventually got wind of it. Seeing his name flash across my screen yet again, I decided to answer it.

"You ol' country muthafucka. I'm ready to fly down there and put another bullet in you!"

"Listen Chinx, I know it looks bad, but trust me, it ain't all that bad."

"How the fuck not when you got the pigs involved?"

"Listen, they don't think the shit is mine."

"I don't care who they think it belongs to, that's my money you playing with."

"I got it handled, give me 24 hours."

"Twelve, or I'm on the next flight out," he ended the call. Knowing I had to be in this bed for a few more days, I had to get in touch with my right hand man out here; if he hadn't already given up all the information. Dialing his number, it rang out until his voicemail picked up. Shooting him a text, I told him to call me ASAP. Closing my phone, I looked at my screensaver, it was a picture of Lucy on our porch in my favorite red dress. The split stopped just above her knee; her hair was bone straight, falling just above her small breasts. She was happy, her smile was bright and the shimmer lip gloss she wore complimented her look. Damn I fucked up; she wasn't just my girl. Lucy was the woman I wanted to marry, the woman I wanted to have my kids. I was throwing dirt on her name trying to buy my ass some time.

Sighing heavily, I shot her a text letting her know I missed her and I was sorry for everything.

She quickly told me to go fuck myself. Laughing at her, I don't know who she was turning into. Lucy was such a sweetheart when I met her, graduating college with a degree in education. She rarely cursed and damn sure wasn't giving me no pussy. I had to force her to drink until I started stressing her out with my mother's antics. I couldn't imagine how much shots she'd taken since the shooting.

Laying my head back on the pillow, the pain killer I had earlier was finally kicking in. Closing my eyes, I kept replaying over and over what had transpired in the house. Shit, if I didn't get robbed, I damn sure was going to run with that story before Chinx thought I had another motive.

8

ASAAD

"Nigga, I'm telling you, I'm going to Raleigh. I'ma get a hotel and when the muthafucka can't deliver, I'ma pop up on his ass!" Chinx shouted into the line. Feeling him getting himself riled up yet again, I told him if he was leaving, I was gonna roll with him. Gabby was beginning to irk my nerves every second I was in her presence. What started out as me only seeing her here and there had turned into her walking on my side of the house more often.

After leaving the bar last night, I wanted to bring Lou back with me, but I knew Gabby was already on some shit. She had been blowing up my line about how I drove away after she caught me smoking in the car. Shit, I had no choice, the bitch complained about the smoke in the house, so what was I supposed to do? Chinx told me to be on standby; to be ready just in case he called. Sitting a few blocks from the house, I looked over at the small bouquet of roses I had picked up. I planned on running into Lucy earlier to drop them off to her, but the nigga she was with clearly had her full attention. Misha tried to explain the situation, but I wasn't hearing it.

Leaning over, I opened up the passenger door and pushed

the roses onto the ground before driving to the house. Pulling into the driveway, I saw Gabby's red Nissan Murano parked in its usual spot. Hopping out, I walked up the driveway. Before I could place my key in the door, it swung open. Gabby was standing there in a hot pink jogging suit with her gray Vapormax on. Her chocolate complexion looked like it was sprayed with coconut oil and her usual 20-inch weave was now pinned up in a high bun. Rolling my head on my neck, I sighed before moving to the side. Expecting Gabby to walk past me, she moved to the side allowing me to come in.

"Where you been Asaad?"

There goes that damn annoying squeaky voice, I thought side eyeing her. "Gabby, don't start your shit with me, aight? We ain't together, so I owe you nothing." Holding up her freshly manicured nails, she displayed the three-carat wedding ring and band I had purchased her two years prior.

"Hello muthafucka, if you haven't realized it, I'm still your wife. I still carry Matthews as my last name so..." Snapping her neck from side to side, looking like the typical bird she was, I dismissed her with the flip of my finger.

"Trust, we won't be married for too much longer if I have my way!" Taking the stairs two at a time, escaping the wrath she was about to unleash.

"Who is she Asaad? I know it's some new bitch that got you thinking ya dick don't stink!" Rummaging through my closet, I grabbed the first two sweat suits and sneakers that matched. She wasn't about to drive me crazy with her bullshit. I wished she had found a nigga in the midst of this separation, because she was really making me look older than 35 right about now.

When I met Gabby, she had shit going for herself, I mean she had it all going for herself. Gabby was a college graduate with an IT degree working for Google. The minute she got word that not only did I have two buildings I was renting out to tenants, I was in the streets with Chinx, she let her job go and did nothing but spend my fucking money. She wasn't trying to give me a kid, hell I'd even take a dog at this point. The home cooked meals stopped, and I was ordering from Uber Eats more.

The bedroom door swung open with Gabby standing in the doorway with a glass of liquor in her hand. *"Fucking drunk yo,"* I mumbled, noticing it was only one in the afternoon.

"Gabby, go lay ya drunk ass down, I'm tired of your raggedy mouth!" Giving her a disapproving look, I picked up my bag of clothes and brushed past her. She was so drunk, she staggered over and fell on the floor spilling her drink.

"I can't stand ya black ass Asaad! I hope the bitch fuck you over like you did me!" Not even addressing her allegations, I walked out the house and got in my car driving off.

Chinx told me to meet him at the airport, he had purchased the fastest tickets to North Carolina. Misha had sent me a text telling me her cousin had mentioned my name. Closing it out without responding, I was over these bitches and their unnecessary drama. Clearly, Lou's fiancé that she wasn't with had popped up on her ass in New York. I wanted no parts of the shit. Sitting at the airport, I spotted Chinx's high yellow ass walking through the airport with a fucking yellow shirt on. This nigga didn't know how to tone it down a bit, hoping his ass ain't have his chain on his neck, I was relieved when I saw him bare.

Getting up, he gave me dap before we headed to TSA. "Yo, I got Ra and them meeting me down there tonight."

"Say less."

9

MISHA

Watching Lou pace back and forth through the hotel room, I could see the worried look on her face. She was huffing and puffing too much for me to keep count. "Girl just relax, your father is not going to let you go to prison."

She looked up and for the first time, I saw the tears running down her face. Her eyes were red and puffy from crying.

"Stop crying girl, you're going to be good."

Choking back her tears, she replied "My father just texted me that because I didn't have the full voice note, Hassel saying that meant nothing." Falling onto the bed, she cried into her hands. I hated to see my little cousin upset like this; it pissed me off. She went the good route; went to school, graduated, got a job and then a fiancé all for him to fuck her over like the pussy he was.

"I honestly don't know shit Misha; you know how my father is." She acts like I don't know how low down Oliver's ass could be. Shit, he hated me for no damn reason. Patting her back trying to soothe her, the door beeped just as Oliver strolled into the room.

"I could have sworn I told your ass to stay away from my daughter, you just don't learn, huh?" Glaring at him with hatred in my eyes he dismissed me. Walking over to where we were, he yanked Lucy off the floor with one tug. "We're going home and you're going to talk to these fucking cops Lucy!"

"I know daddy, I told you I understood." Jumping back before Oliver could strike Lou, she flinched. Side eyeing her, I'd make sure to go straight to my mother after I left here because he was getting too loose with his hands. I know Lou told me he had popped her mouth earlier, but shit, he was giving me abusive vibes. Not looking at me twice, Lucy followed him out of the room. Once the door was closed, I pulled out my phone waiting on my mother to answer.

"Ma!"

"Girl, it better be a damn emergency, yelling in my fucking ear while I'm watching my show!"

"Argh, it is. What's the deal with Oliver's ass?" Never addressing him as my uncle, the phone grew silent.

"What are you referring to child?"

"Ma, I think he over there beating on Lucy, and you know she all small like auntie."

"Misha stay out of that drama; I can't stand that man and the minute he come barking up the wrong tree I'ma give him something he's not going to like." Sighing heavily, I headed out the room and down towards the elevator. If my mother said to drop it, I had no choice but to drop it.

"Fine ma, but I'm telling you if she calls me crying again I'ma make a trip out there."

"Over my dead body Misha, now drop it!" my mother spat sternly before telling me to come by the house.

"Okay, I'm on my way." Keeping my phone on loud, I made sure to listen for any texts or calls from Lou because I was going to her side whether my mother approved of it or not. I grew up as an only child, just like she did. Before my aunt Lyla was murdered me and Lou were always together. Although she lived in North Carolina and I stayed up here in New York, we were super close. After my aunt died, I remember my mother and Oliver had a fight about her keeping Lou and raising her, but he wouldn't budge.

Hopping into the Uber I ordered, I looked down at the messages from Don asking if he could come holla at me. The nigga only wanted to holla when he needed to get his dick wet. I was tired of him and all these niggas. The money was getting slimmer fucking with these dudes, so it wasn't like I was living the lavish life anyway. I had recently run into Chinx, Asaad's boy a few days back and he told me he wanted to come see me.

That was a dude I was willing to stick in the game for. His pockets were heavy and he wasn't no cheap nigga. He used to fuck with Dazzle, who stripped in Queens for a few years, so I knew he wasn't no stranger to my lifestyle. Laying my head back on the black leather seat, I closed my eyes for a few minutes.

Pulling up at my mother's building, I hopped out. Walking to 314 and 143rd street, I yelled up for her to send one of the boys down. Yeah, I know it was ghetto but hell, they locked the doors in this fucking project without distributing the damn keys.

"Ma, grandma went to the store!" I heard my son yell from the park known as the square. He was hanging on the gate looking like somebody's lost child with no home training.

"Boy get down and bring ya ass over here then." Waving for him and his brother to come meet me at the sidewalk so we could wait for my mother in front of the building, I heard her yapping to her neighbor.

"Now I know I told you I was on my way ma."

"And, you act like I went someplace far." Stopping at the black gate, she said, "I was just at the firehouse, relax." For it to be the middle of May, it was hotter than usual in New York.

Walking ahead of her to the apartment, I filled her in on the details of what was going on. Rolling her eyes, she told me Oliver was a fucking trip and he was holding Lou hostage to feel like he was doing something right.

"You know he feels responsible for Lyla's murder that's why he was so hard on Lou."

"But still ma, she's grown and he's still treating her like a kid."

"Trust me, that girl gonna snap soon, I just hope I'm there when it happens."

"Yeah."

"Where's her no good fiancé?"

"He's the one who got her mixed up in this shit." Smacking her lips, my mother ended the conversation, getting up to go and make lunch. Leaving me to drop it as well.

10

LOU

BACK IN RALEIGH

The flight back to Raleigh was fast; yet draining. Between my father giving me the third degree and trashing my brand new BMW, I was over it all. I wished I could get in touch with Asaad, but I guess he was still hung up on his wife. How the hell could he damn near seduce me in a public bathroom and then run bank to his wife? Tuh, he was more of a bitch than I thought. With my music on blast and my eyes closed tightly, I tuned out my annoying father. I knew the minute I stepped foot in North Carolina I was going to fuck up Hassel, I didn't give a damn if he was on his death bed.

He not only pissed my father off, but he spread dirt on my name forgetting that I was an elementary school teacher. My damn livelihood was at stake because he wanted to play with the big boys while still sucking on his mama titty.

The tapping on my leg made me open my eyes slightly. Removing the air pods from my ears, I asked my father what he wanted.

"We are about to land."

Thanks for staying the obvious, I thought. I felt the plane landing, I wasn't stupid.

"I'm aware, I'm just trying to get as much sleep as I can before I go to hell." With sarcasm dripping from my voice, I knew he dared to not hit me in public.

Leaning over in his seat he said, "Lucy don't play with me." Shrugging him off, I waited for the plane to fully land before following behind him. As usual, there was a car waiting for us to take us to the station and talk.

"Dad, if I told you I had nothing to do with this, why am I going to the station?"

"To clear your damn name." I ain't never been a snitch and I wasn't about to start snitching now.

"Whatever, let's get this over with." Riding in silence the whole drive to the station when I got inside, I was met with some of the familiar officers I know. One of them happened to be a guy who had been trying to holla for the past five years. Sighing heavily, I followed behind them into the room.

"Listen Lucy, we know you're innocent, but there's no way we can pin this on your fiancé without the right amount of evidence." I didn't know what they were looking for, shit, I wasn't even listed on the house yet. Walking into the room I flopped down into the chair, thinking they needed to make this quick.

"Listen, I know how this goes, my father was a cop and then a judge, so let's not beat around the bush here," I said, letting them know I wasn't a stranger to the interrogation room. "You want me to say something I know nothing about, I'm not listed on Hassel's house and my fingerprints are not on either of the weapons that were found at the scene."

"We know all that Lucy, what we don't know is why would he be dealing drugs as the pastor?"

"I don't know, I wish I got a warning cuz I would have stayed with my ex-boyfriend for all that!"

Sitting back in my chair, I folded my arms across my chest. "Can y'all check my hands for gun residue, so I can get out of here?" Fed up with them playing games with me, I cut straight to the chase.

"We can't let you go; you were at the scene of a crime."

"So why the hell that bastard don't have cops at his room, or better yet why isn't his bitch ass arrested?" Glaring at them matter of factly, I answered my own question, "Oh wait, y'all must be on his payroll, huh?"

Slamming his fist on the metal table, I jumped back a bit.

"Must be true." Tilting my head to the side, I replied, "Can I get a lawyer if I'm being charged with a crime?"

"Lucy go ahead, but just know if you're mixed up in that bullshit with him, you're going down."

"I'll do you one better, if I'm mixed up in it, I'll turn myself in." Smirking in his direction, I winked before leaving out of the room. I could hear them talking as I left out. Shrugging them off, I walked swiftly through the station and out the door. My father was on my heels, I could hear his hard bottom shoes walk across the pavement. Stopping short, I turned on my heels to face him, "Dad, I'm going to the hospital to see Hassel, whether you like it or not!" The look on his face showed he was disgusted in me, but I paid it no mind. I was over him and his controlling ways, as well as him treating me more like a criminal than a victim.

"You're going where?"

"To the hospital, I'm clearing my name and that's what it is." Walking into the street, I looked down the road to see if any cars were coming my way. Had this been New York, taxis would have been lined up, but I was back home in this country ass town.

"Get in the damn car!" my father ordered as he pointed to his navy blue Lexus. Rolling my head on my shoulders, I would have rather hop in an Uber but I needed to get to this hospital as soon as I could. Hassel had played too many games with running my name through the mud. Hopping into my father's car that he left at the station, I tuned him out as I thought of how I was going to approach Hassel. I wanted to walk in and slap him but then again, I didn't know if his annoying, holier than thou mother was in attendance. Biting my bottom lip I silently prayed that I got an epiphany before I pulled up there.

11

HASSEL

Laid up watching another rerun of Law & Order SVU, I smirked at how Olivia had outsmarted yet another rapist. "Fucking stupid," I mumbled just as I heard the door push open. Rubbing my tongue across my teeth, I was looking directly at my plug Chinx and his infamous boss. He walked in grabbing a chair and pulling it up to my bedside.

Sitting on it with the back facing me, he said, "So, you mind telling me what the fuck happened with my product?"

Throwing up my hands in my own defense, I watched the other guy who stared at me with the coldest eyes. Expecting him to sit like Chinx, he stood by my bedside burning a hole in me.

"Listen, I told you I got robbed and them niggas shot me."

"You also said ya bitch ass fiancé was there and she set the shit up, right?"

"I don't know if she set it up but she was definitely there," I wasn't trying to fuck Lucy over with these types of niggas. I could tell Chinx's partner was about his business. He looked like a killer and the gun he had on his waistband was noticeable. How the fuck he got that shit out here? As fast as Chinx got here, I'm sure he flew down from New York.

"So, where is she?" Chinx asked, looking around the plain hospital room. I didn't have any security on my room and my nigga was gone for the day. Hearing shuffling in the hallway, I heard Lucy's voice in the distance. I could have been dreaming, when you staring death right in the face, you tend to make up shit in your head, so I didn't know.

Lucy swung open the door with force and a scowl plastered on her face. "Hassel, you got some fucking nerve with your pussy ass!" That's all I heard before all eyes were on my fiancé. The look of shock on her face when she looked over at Chinx and his partner didn't go unnoticed. She froze, I could have sworn she had stopped breathing as she glared into that nigga's cold eyes.

"Lucy what are you doing here?" I wanted to cause a distraction between their obvious attraction.

12

ASAAD

Seeing her in the flesh looking at me, only a few feet away, had my mouth dry. I wanted to grab her small ass up and drag her into the hallway, but here I was in a room with her and three other niggas around. Never moving my hand from my waistband, her eyes trailed down my chest, landing on my nine in my pants. Blinking her eyes, she swallowed hard while Chinx and the nigga Has went back and forth about the bricks that were missing. The dude from the parking lot earlier was standing there with a perplexed look on his face.

"Fuck is going on here?" I managed to say, never removing my eyes from Lou.

"So y'all the fucking criminals who Hassel working under, huh?" The dude with Lou asked. She waved him off and told him to shush. Turning to face Hassel, she walked closer to him. Bending down, she drew her hand back slapping him across the face.

I'm sure I saw the spit flying from his mouth as he looked on with wrinkles in forehead.

"To think I was going to marry you! You planted them drugs on me to get off scot free, huh?" she shouted in a fit of rage, finally catching on that she was engaged to Hassel and not the other dude, I could have kicked myself.

"Yo Chinx, fuck this pussy ass pastor who clearly ain't built for this life."

Lou stormed out of the room just as the older dude reached out for her.

"Dad I'm done," was all she said as she left out of the room. Turning my head in that direction, I wanted to run after her but I couldn't leave Chinx.

Lou and her father were gone, leaving us alone with Hassel. Chinx walked up on him, punching him in the face. Blood spilled from the split in his lip. "You will be released soon. I'ma be back, but it looks like my nigga's feeling ya fiancé, so we gotta go." Leaving out the hospital, I searched the parking lot for a sign of Lou anywhere.

"Nigga, so that's the bitch you open off, huh?"

"Don't call her out her name; Lou is her name," I corrected him still looking around just as I saw her arguing with her father before sitting in the passenger seat. "Aight, follow that damn Lexus, Chinx." Getting in the car, I watched Chinx weave in and out of traffic keeping up with Lou. I wasn't about to lose her little ass again, I let her get away in New York, but this town was small.

"I can't believe this muthafucka really tried to pin that shit on his fiancé." Licking my bottom lip, I held my hand up to my beard rubbing it annoyed. Finally catching up to where Lou and her father were, I saw her fall out of the moving car.

"The fuck!"

13
____

LOU

"TEN MINUTES BEFORE; STAY OR JUMP."

"I'm tired of you disrespecting me Lucy! First, you take your ass to New York, then you up in the hospital showing your ass!" Glancing over at my over dramatic father, I must have rolled my eyes one to many times. The slap across my face caught me off guard. On an instinct, I drew my hand back slapping him in the center of his face. The car swerved in traffic as my eyes widened with shock. Before he could react and steal off on me, I removed my seatbelt and hopped out of the moving car.

Reaching out my hands to brace my fall, they scraped against the cement. Seeing the blood pour from my nail, I rolled over onto the side of the road behind a parked car. Gripping my hand, I closed my eyes, trying to steady my heavy breathing. My chest heaved up and down. Laying my head back on the car, my adrenaline rushed as I shot up to go run before my father came after me.

"Lucy, I'ma fuck you up!" I heard him shout. Walking in the opposite direction, I walked right into Asaad's open arms.

"You ain't doing shit, so get back in the fucking car old

man." With my face buried in Asaad's chest, I prayed my father listened to him.

"Who the fuck you think you talking to?" Hearing the bass in my father's voice that I hadn't heard in years made me push Asaad back a little.

"Please Asaad, just go," I whispered, praying he heard me.

"Only if you're coming with me." Looking down at me, I nodded my head. I had to get away from my father, if I could call him that right about now.

"Lucy, if you go with that thug ass nigga, don't bring your ass back when he cheat or beat on you!" Coming down from my adrenaline rush, I didn't look back as I went to limp off. Asaad turned on his heels and grabbed me up, carrying me to the car. The pain was starting to take over. Wincing in his arms I looked down at my legs, which were covered in blood splatter.

"Are you crazy, Lou? You could have seriously hurt yourself." Unable to speak, I closed my eyes tightly to stop the tears and pain. Holding me tight, his boy opened the door. Once I was laid across the back seat, I asked him if he could stop to get me some tissue and pain killers.

"Yeah, no doubt, I'm still pissed at how the fuck you jump from a moving car Lucy." The way he said my name sent chills down my spine and the hair on my arm stand up. Nodding my head, I closed my eyes as my breathing steadied.

"Yo, so you serious 'bout this bro?" Chinx asked him like I wasn't lying in the backseat.

"I said she's coming with me, right? What else I gotta say?" Smiling inwardly, I loved how he took up for me without question.

Dozing off, I was awakened to the car stopping. Popping my eyes open on instinct, I tried to sit up quickly, forgetting my aching legs. "Fuck!" I cried out in pain, falling back into the seat.

"Lou Relax, Assad went to get you some shit for ya leg." Turning my head to the side, I looked at Chinx. He was a lighter complexion, with long locs pulled into a ponytail. He must have been about 6 '3 in height, not as built as Assad, but you could tell he wasn't no slouch. Staring at his back, I continued to look out the window dismissing my vibrating phone.

"Why is it taking him so long in the store?" I mumbled, hoping Chinx ain't hear me. He turned around and told me he wasn't into no foul play.

Assad strolled out of the store on his cellphone. Whoever it was must of had him fucked up, the wrinkles on his head and the way he barked on the caller, I would have hated to be them.

"Yo Chinx, come holla at me. Here Lou, get ya self-cleaned up." Tossing the bag in the backseat, I moved my leg just in time to miss the bag hitting it. Rolling my eyes and shaking my head, I now contemplated if I wanted to be up under Assad.

"So what you doing with this nigga? Al said he went to the hospital and the muthafucka ain't there no more." Peeking through the tinted windows, I watched Asaad closely.

"His bitch in the fucking car, get the damn address, my nigga!" Chinx paced the dirt road back and forth. "How much you feeling shorty, cuz I mean we could—" before Chinx could suggest something, Assad shut him down.

"I'm not mixing Lou up in shit. I'm trying to get her ass away from them and you want to send her to them." Shaking his head, he said, "Check this out, I'ma get us a room, and then we can go get up with Al."

"Aight, no doubt." Seeing them head back in the direction of the car, I opened the alcohol pack and placed it on my leg. Screaming out in agony, Assad pulled the door back.

"What the fuck?"

"It burns, I mean that's obvious; it's alcohol." Forcing a smile on my face to stop from tearing up.

"Just leave it alone, put the tissue on it until I get you in a room." Following his lead, I just looked through the notifications on my phone. Jen and Misha were the only people I was responding to. Jen wanted to know where I was and if I needed to come stay with her for a few days, but I knew that wouldn't be a good idea.

Misha told me to bring my ass back to New York and she would protect me. I didn't know how cuz she was not going to go up against my father.

Pulling into a Holiday Inn hotel, I waited until Assad told me what room we were going to be in. I wasn't sure if I'd be sleeping alone or with him, but hell, I know I needed a few shots of cognac to fall out. Opening the car I hopped out, leaning up against the car. I couldn't shake this pain shooting up in my leg. At this moment, I couldn't stand my father.

"Why you get out the car, Lou? Niggas probably looking for you and you in plain sight."

"Sorry, I just didn't want to sit in there alone." Looking down at the ground, I stared at my sneakers instead of his face.

Assad lifted my chin with his hand, "Look at me when I'm talking to you, Lou." Batting my lashes in his direction, for the first time, I really got a good look at this handsome man in the light. His complexion was a light caramel, he had a dimple on his left cheek and his full beard had some blonde strands in it. Moving a loose curl from my face, Asaad asked if I could walk on my own. Not wanting to seem like a nag, I told him I had it, just walk slow.

"You just gotta be hardcore, huh?" he asked, swooping me up in his arms. Laying my head against his chest, I melted in his arms. "Exactly, let me take care of your ass."

Chuckling, I buried my face in his hoodie, hiding from the people in the hotel. Once I was in the room, he placed me on my feet. "I got the room right there, I'ma go handle some shit, but I'm leaving my card for you to order some food." I know the look of disappointment on my face was evident. "You gon' be good?"

"Yeah." Taking the card from his hand, I looked away. "Can I get a drink?"

"Get what you need Lou, gimme ya phone, so I can get your number." Reaching in my back pocket, I pulled out my iPhone. Handling it to him, he put his number in it, seeing my screen light up with a number he saved it. Handing the phone back to me, Assad used the key to open the door. Once I was in the room and he turned to leave. I looked away.

Here I was melting over a dude I knew nothing about except he got me open and he saved me. "Gimme a kiss, Lou." Shit, he was demanding yet so sexy doing it. Bending down, he grabbed my chin before kissing my lips. A slight moan escaped my lips.

"Listen, hit my line for anything, aight lil' mama?"

"Aight." Watching him leave out the door, I limped further into the room. Ordering food and a bottle of Jack Daniels, I got in a quick shower before bandaging my leg.

14

———

HASSEL

"Shit!" I mumbled hopping out of the bed. I had to get away from that hospital before Chinx and his boss came back to pay me a visit. I was pissed off that Lucy was clearly fucked up over his boy and praying Oliver took her to his house. I knew them New York dudes were ruthless; they would hurt anyone just to get back at someone. Calling up my mother, I told her to meet me at the Red Roof plus hotel. I needed a rundown place cuz I knew them niggas wouldn't check there, Lucy knew I liked the finer things, so if she was dealing with the dude, she wouldn't think I was there.

Holding my side and limping to the elevator, I felt someone glaring at me. Looking around, nobody I came across looked familiar. Shrugging off the feeling I got in the elevator, pulling out my phone I ordered an Uber to the hotel. Waiting in the entrance of the hospital, I dialed Lucy's number only for it to ring out until her voicemail picked up. Cursing myself, I called her father's number.

"Hassel what do you want?" Oliver stressed into the line.

"Listen, I'm trying to see if Lucy is with you. I'm worried about her."

"Bullshit, you ain't worried about my daughter muthafucka. You're worried she's laid up with the next muthafucka!"

I mean he was right, but I wasn't about to let the cocky muthafucka know that.

"Listen, I know I was fucked up to her but she's still my fiancé!"

"Fuck the bullshit Hassel, she ain't marrying your criminal ass!" He took a deep breath. "I done told you I didn't want her around the shit and at your rate you're headed to jail." Ending the call in my ear, I was livid. Oliver always let his ego get the best of him, but if he knew like I knew he better tread lightly. I knew more shit about him that he thought I didn't.

Sitting in the Uber until he pulled up at the hotel, I continued to call Lucy. Failing every time, I wanted to toss my phone but I knew I needed it. Hopping outside, I saw my mother standing by her car waving in my direction, looking over my shoulder, I limped towards her.

"Why would you leave the hospital without getting discharged?"

"Ma, some guys came to see me and they threatened me." If I had told her the full story, she probably wouldn't be standing here right now.

"They wanted to kill you?" The look on her face told me my mother knew more about the streets then she claimed.

Following behind her to the hotel, I took a mental note to check her later about her not being surprised. For as long as I could remember, my mother was a church going woman who did nothing wrong, but the look in her eyes today told me otherwise. Once in the room, I staggered to the bathroom to change my dressing. The vibration on my phone showed up with Chinx's name displayed on the screen. Silencing the call, another one followed through. Knowing I needed to get to the bottom of the call, I heard what sounded like the hotel door bursting open.

"Oh my god, Hassel!" was all I heard my mother shout before I heard footsteps in the distance.

Tip toeing to the bathroom door, it busted open before a hand yanked me out. "This pussy was about to let his mother go down!" Hearing the familiar voice, I tried to look over my shoulder. The barrel of the nine came crashing down on my head. On instinct, I dropped to the floor, reaching for the dude over my head, he twisted my hand behind me. Dragging me out the motel and onto the streets. I looked on in horror.

"Nigga, so you was really trying to escape?"

Looking up at Chinx, he shrugged as Asaad looked down on me in disgust. "You owe my bro some bread and a brick, so what's the word?"

Lifting my hands up in my defense, I wasn't about to lose my life over coke that I clearly got robbed for. They didn't know the truth, and with everyone either dead or nearly dead, I was running with this story.

"Listen, let me explain what's going on."

"Nigga, I didn't come here for an explanation; I'm trying to get back to the spot with my shorty and chop it up." The smirk on his face told me he was doing some foul shit.

"I get that, but I was robbed." I didn't see the blow to my face coming but I damn sure felt it. Falling over to the ground, he bent down beside me, "Who set your ass up?"

Holding my lip, I replied, "Nigga, I don't know."

Laughing, Chinx looked away. Seeing the spit forming in the corner of his mouth, I looked up at Asaad who was leaning on the wall smoking a blunt. These niggas were ruthless to say the least.

"You better get me my money Hass or your sweet old mom gonna see the light before her time!" Furrowing my brows and twisting up my lips, I agreed to his terms. I couldn't get my mother mixed up in this bullshit. Grabbing me up off the ground, Chinx told me I had 'til tonight to get him his fifty thousand or else. I didn't even want to know what the *or else* was.

Watching them walk away, I placed a call to my mother. "Ma listen, these guys ain't no good. I gotta get them their money or they coming for you."

"Coming for me? I ain't mixed up in your mess, Hassel."

"Ma it ain't that damn simple." I was vexed with how callous she was acting.

"I survived the shit with your father and here it is, you just had to go down that route!" Ending the call in my ear, I was thrown off by what she said.

Stumbling up the stairs, I headed to the room. Walking in, I spotted my mother holding a duffle bag.

"How much money do you need Hassel?" she asked looking at me in my face. The sweat suit and sneakers she wore took away from her sweet look. Her usually curly hair was pulled back into a tight bun.

"Ma, I don't need you going into your savings."

"Boy, don't worry about where I'm going for the money, just give me the damn amount!"

Raising her voice louder than usual, she placed her hand on her hips. "Hassel, I have some stuff I need to tell you, but when the time is right. Go get yourself cleaned up so you can pay these dudes."

Squinting my eyes in her direction, I walked into the bathroom. Seeing she had a pair of dark jogging pants and matching jacket for me already in there, I got showered and dressed.

15

———

MISHA

Pacing my apartment back and forth, I tried calling Lou again. When her phone rang out to the voicemail, I dialed her father's number.

"Misha, what do you want?"

"Oliver, right about now I don't care if you like me or not. I want to know where my cousin is!" Demanding he give me an answer, I was ready to risk it all for her.

"Misha, I don't know where she is, she went with them niggas who are after Hassel." Hearing the stress in his voice for the first time in a long time, I knew he really didn't know.

"So, you just let her leave, huh?" Rolling my eyes to the ceiling, I blew air out of my mouth. "Stupid muthafucka!"

"Lyla please!" he stopped short confusing me, "I mean Misha, you think I wouldn't just let my daughter walk away with some no good niggas?"

"Why did you call me Lyla?"

"Nothing Misha, I'm tired and I need my baby girl to come home safe."

"She texted me and told me she leapt from your car."

Sighing heavily, he cleared his throat. I sat on the sofa,

placing my phone on speaker. "She did jump from the car Misha, I smacked her and she hit me back, then she jumped."

"What?"

"Listen, aight, you think I like hitting her?"

"Yeah, I do, cuz your ass do that a lot. I'm kinda happy she's with Asaad." Tapping my foot impatiently, against the tiled floor. "She needs a real dude to love her cuz all you've been doing is hitting her and that punk ass fiancé she was about to marry was nothing but a lying asshole."

"You're right Misha, shit I know." Breathing as if I was annoying him, he said, "You sound more like your mother every day."

"Your point?"

"Damn, I miss her."

Furrowing my brows in confusion, I asked, "You miss my mother?"

"Listen, do new a favor Misha, get ahold of Lou. We need to have a sit down."

"You're gonna tell me what this shit is about, right?"

"Not until I get in touch with my baby girl. Anyway, I gotta meet up with someone." The call ended before I could respond to him. Pissed off with the fact that I still got nowhere, I scrolled through my call log where I found Chinx's number stored.

Sending him a message, I asked if he could talk.

Chinx: now isn't a good time. Give me a few

Me: copy, can you tell Asaad to hit me up about Lou?

Chinx: Aight.

Less than five minutes had passed and Asaad was calling my line, "Yo, is Lou good?"

"I'm not sure cuz she's not answering my calls or texts, and her father wants her home."

"Shit, aight stay by ya phone. I'ma go check on her."

"Okay cool, if I don't answer just send me a text."

"No, you better fucking answer Misha, on god!"

Throwing my hands up in my defense, I told him I'd keep the phone on loud. When he got off the line, I sent yet another text to Lou before getting in the shower. Stepping out of the tub I dried off, stopping at my mid-section. I looked down at the tiger stripes on my stomach. Sucking my teeth, I was happy I didn't have much of a gut, but these marks always turned me off about my body. Hearing my phone ring on the sink, I grabbed it up hoping it was a message from Asaad. Instead it was Chinx.

Chinx: when I get back, I'm trying to see you

Me: no problem. You good?

Chinx: yea I'm good shorty.

I don't know why I asked was he good, I mean I knew he was down south cuz he had shit to handle. The instinct in me wanted to make sure he wasn't hurt or dead. Placing the phone back down, I wanted to respond to him, but I knew what it was between me and him. Chinx wasn't about to wife me up, so I had to put my feelings aside and get money.

Getting dressed, I called my mother's line, "Girl, it better be an emergency. You know my show is on." She was always watching some damn show.

"Ma it is important, Oliver did something weird today that got me wondering some things."

Hearing her sigh, I figured she was probably going to brush me off. "What did that asshole say?"

"Well first, he called me Aunty's name and second he's like he needs to talk to me and Lou about something."

"Fuck him, you ain't gotta talk to him about shit." Blowing out into the line, my mother was probably smoking on a Newport 100 cigarette.

"I'm just saying ma why would he—" Cutting me off, she told me to leave well enough alone. Dropping the conversation, I decided to go search for my half smoked blunt I left in the ashtray.

16

ASAAD

"Yo, I'm ready to kill this muthafucka and get back to New York!" I said, sitting in the car running my hand over my matted beard. I needed a shower, a hot meal and to lay up under Lou. Getting the separate rooms was more for her than it was for me. I knew I wanted her little ass the minute she tried to cut me, but she clearly had ties to a nigga I needed dead.

"Nigga, you just trying to lay up under that country ass pussy." Chinx started laughing. Side eyeing him, I wasn't the least bit amused.

"What the fuck ever, just handle this shit cuz last I checked, you trying to smash her cousin."

"You damn right, I don't know why you ain't tried in all them years you been renting out that apartment to her."

"Nigga, now you know my pops and her mother are cool. You think I wanted beef with the nigga?"

"Yeah, you right, cuz Frankie would fuck you up if you mess with Misha." Sitting back in the car, I texted Lou to see if she was good. She responded back that she was sleep, so I left her alone. Letting Misha know she was good, I told Chinx to open up the small bottle of Hennessy.

We had been in North Carolina for a few hours and I now understand why I hate it here. It was too slow and these niggas was dumb. Hassel swore he was going to run game, telling us he was robbed by some random ass niggas when Chinx and I knew exactly who set him up. The only fucked up shit is the fact he wasn't supposed to live through it. When Chris told me there was a chick in the crib, I could have killed him myself. We had been using Chris against Hassel for the longest because he thought he was the man who would become a pastor and still handle the streets.

When Chris told us he was slipping big time, moving in his shorty and flashing money and cars, Chinx said we had to handle him. The fact that we wanted to expand down south, we knew our young boy Chris was well connected. The minute we got word that he was being sloppy we told Chris to go take him out. Chris called us when he heard the shots rang out. He sent two of his flunkies in the house and neither of them came out good. The one who survived was in the hospital on the same floor as Hassel.

"Yo nigga, what you trying to do?" Chinx pulled me back from my thoughts, flashing his phone in my face. The video on the screen disgusted me. Turning up my lip, I snatched the phone from his hand, looking at Gabby enter my room with bleach in her hands, throwing it on my clothing and shoes. I wanted to get back to New York and strangle the life out of her. The fact her dumbass recorded it and posted it on her Instagram story told me the bitch was out of her mind. Saving the video to Chinx's phone I sent it to me directly.

"She fucking losing it bro, if I go and knock her the fuck out, I'll be wrong."

"Nah, sis wildin' out there but just go make the divorce final my nigga."

That shit was easier said than done. If I could keep up with her for the next six months, the house resell for sixty thousand more than what we paid. We said we were going to go that route and split the money. When we moved in, Gabby was working and contributed to the house, so I wasn't about to be a dick head and shit on her completely, but she was making me rethink that.

Taking the bottle of Hennessy from Chinx, I turned it over taking a huge gulp. "Chinx let's get this muthafucka Hassel, cuz. I'm already wasting enough fucking time as it is!"

"Say less." Starting up the car, Chinx called Chris to see where Hassel's mother lived. Once we got word on it, we headed to the house. Pulling up the block, we sat outside for a good two hours before I grew annoyed.

"This nigga ain't coming home, gimme a minute." Stepping outside the car, I called Lou,

"Yo!" Hearing her answer in a groggily tone, I dismissed the fact she was sleeping.

"Do me a favor, that nigga been reaching out to you, right?"

"Yeah, why?"

"I ain't got time for the questions Lou, call the nigga and tell him to meet you right now!" Putting some extra bass in my voice, she had to understand how serious I was.

"Okay, am I giving him this address, Asaad?" she asked in a hesitant tone. I'd explain to her later, but right now I needed her to help me out.

"Yeah, tell him to come to the hotel. You ain't gotta give him the room number, but make the shit look good and tell him you need him."

"But, Asaad—" I cut her off with a grunt.

"Lou, just do what the fuck I ask, damn! You starting to get on my nerves." After the words left my mouth, I wanted to take the shit back. Gabby and this nigga Hassel was stressing me the fuck out.

"Fine Asaad, I'll text you when it's done," she ended the call without another word. Sending her a text apologizing, she read the message without responding. Hitting the top of the car, Chinx rolled the window down.

"Nigga this is a fucking rental, be easy bro."

"Yeah, my bad." Treading up and down the block waiting on Lou, I saw her name go across my screen. Relieved, I picked up when she told me he was on his way.

17

HASSEL

"Hassel, that bitch ain't in no trouble, she with her father and I'm sure he wants to lock you up," my mother fussed to my back while I started throwing on the sweat suit. Placing my feet in the black construction Timbs, I pulled the duffle bag my other had. Opening it up, I saw a bunch of cash stacked inside.

"What is this?"

"Don't question me, you said you needed money, so I got you some money."

"Ma where the fuck you get this money?" Unable to control myself, I looked up at her standing with her hands folded across her chest.

"You think I know all about the street shit from television? Your father, June, used to run the block when we met Hassel."

Standing there with my mouth wide open, I had to question who I was talking to. My parents had never displayed that they were in the streets. They acted as if they knew nothing about it.

"So, you had this money stashed away for what, a rainy fucking day?" Turned off by my mother, I grabbed up the bag storming out of the room. Hearing her footsteps behind me, I turned on my heels. "You ain't coming with me!"

"The hell I ain't Hassel, I'm not about to lose you like I lost your father." The shit she was saying was now making sense to me.

My father was killed trying to break up a fight at one of the gas stations a few years back. Now, I'm here questioning if the shit was true or not. Shaking my head, I told her to wait in the room for me.

"Hassel, I'm going with you. I don't trust that little bitch at all."

"Ma, did you forget I'm the one who got her mixed up in this shit? I owe it to her to go make sure she's safe. Then I'ma go meet up with Chinx and get the fuck on."

"I'm coming, I'll get in my car and follow behind you." Looking down at the time, I was running out of hours to go meet up with Chinx. Trying to be levelheaded, I just told her to do what she wanted to do. Popping a Motrin and drinking bottled water, I walked hastily to the car. Calling Lucy, I wanted her to be outside waiting on me.

"Lucy, you outside in the back, right?"

"Yeah Hassel, just don't take long please, I'm not sure how long they're going to be gone."

"Don't worry Lucy, I'm coming." Sitting in the car, I reached over to check my glove compartment. Once I saw my nine was secured, I pulled off. I know I told my mother to follow behind me, but I was trying to lose her quick.

The drive to the hotel was only a few minutes. Checking my rearview mirror, I didn't see my mother's white Benz in sight. Figuring she got lost following behind me, I mouthed "Thank god". Praying to God that she didn't catch up, because if Lucy was playing then my mother would be spared. Driving into the parking lot, it was dark outside, so I had to squint to see where the hell she was standing. Lucy had told me she had on a white shirt and gray sweats; she wasn't dark, so it wouldn't be hard to find her. Driving around back, I saw her leaning up against the brick wall. She had her hands in her pants pocket looking off. Her usually curly hair was pulled up in a high messy bun. "Damn she so gorgeous," I mumbled, rolling down my window to whistle at her. She looked at me shaking her head, coming closer to the car. I put it in park.

"Get in," motioning for her to come around the passenger seat, I turned looking in her direction. Feeling the cold steel on the back of my head, I sucked my teeth. "You stupid bitch! You set me up?" Flaring my nostrils, I looked at the glove compartment and then back at her, just as Chinx grabbed her up. Covering her mouth, he told her to shut up. "Shit!" Thinking Lucy set me up, I realized I had got her deeper in this shit.

"Get the fuck out Hassel. Make a swift move and I swear I will blow your fucking head off!"

"Man, I got the fucking money, just let her go!" Shouting hoping they would listen, the look on Lucy's face was calm, trying to read her expression she looked away.

"Get out." Hearing the gun cock, I reached for the door. Using my hand, I pushed the door open and ducked, hitting Asaad in his leg. He accidentally hit the trigger, letting a shot fly through the car and out the window of the passenger seat. Hearing Lucy gasp, her eyes widened in shock, as she griped her stomach. *This muthafucka shot Lou, what the fuck?* Panic had set in when I looked into her eyes full of fright.

"Fuck!" Jumping out of the car, I went to run away from the scene. Asaad sent shot after shot, hitting me in my right leg, stumbling, I dragged my body to go hide. Turning around, Asaad sent two shots in my chest. Falling on my back, I looked at the dark sky. I could have sworn I saw a few stars and heard my mother calling my name. My chest heaved up and down with a speed I couldn't keep up with.

Blinking my eyes, I shut them tight. Saying a silent prayer to keep Lucy and my mother safe, I opened my eyes to see Chinx standing over me. Staring down the barrel of the nine, I slowed my breathing as Chinx let off two shots. Turning my head to the side, I saw Asaad holding onto Lucy for dear life before everything went black.

18

LOU

"If this is what hell felt like, I wanted to come back to earth."

Hearing footsteps running across the ground, I couldn't focus. I needed to get up, I wanted to get up, but I felt stuck. Looking into Assad's eyes I wanted to tell him to get the fuck off of me. What part of the plan was it for me to get hemmed up by Chinx? That shit wasn't mentioned to me, and the fact that they kept playing cat and mouse with Hassel fucked up my head even more. Here I was on the ground, trying to catch my breath, fighting for my fucking life, and that's when I overheard the two shots. Holding back the tears, I knew it was Hassel meeting his maker.

"Lou, I'm so sorry! I'm so fucking sorry!"

"I want my dad, call my daddy!" Crying out for the very man who had just beat me earlier was insane.

"Yo, we gotta get her to the hospital and quick!" Chinx shouted running in our direction. Lifting me up, they carried me to the car. Laying across the back seat, Asaad jumped in, placing my head in his lap.

"Lou, you gonna be good, I'ma get you some help." My hands gripped my stomach, the fire felt like it was burning a hole in me. Wanting to close my eyes and wake up in my bed, I knew this was my fucking reality. *The fuck was I thinking, sticking around these hood ass niggas,* I thought as I closed my eyes. Asaad's breathing picked up as he rummaged through his phone. "Damn, it was a fucking accident, I swear!'

"Yo, Misha you gotta get down here and quick, Lou got shot." Hearing shouting from the other end, I couldn't make out what she was saying, but I knew it wasn't anything nice. Chinx was driving like a mad man, the shifting of my body and the rocks we were driving over had me feeling like the bullet was ripping through me.

"Lou, I'm sorry ma, that shit wasn't supposed to happen! Yo!" Tuning him out, I couldn't make out what he was saying, I just saw his mouth moving a mile a minute.

Was this what death felt like? Would I finally see my mother again? The car came to an abrupt stop, Chinx jumped out returning in a few seconds with a doctor.

"Is she alert?" I heard them ask, as I was lifted onto a gurney.

Asaad grabbed my hand in his before asking me to forgive him. Before I could answer, I got a good look at him, the tears were running down his face and his eyes were red and puffy from crying. Closing my eyes, I couldn't look at him anymore. Being pushed away, he yelled for me to believe him.

I wasn't in love, hell I barely knew him. He had shot me less than five feet away. I could die, I could have a fucking shit bag for the rest of my life. What if I couldn't have kids? I was in my twenties; this was not the life I wanted. I left my fiancé and witnessed his murder all because I ran into the arms of a nigga who was no good. He was angry, shit the nigga was bipolar if you ask me. Before the shooting, his ass was yelling at me to go along with the plan, next he's here talking about forgive him, he's sorry. Drifting in and out of full consciousness, I slipped away.

I was back in the gas station, backing up when I was cut off. The minute I jumped out of the car, I wanted to release the anger; grabbing my knife and lunging forward. "Shit, he was so damn handsome," I mumbled, but still he had tried to kill me. The cocky grin on his face, the way he walked; reaching for him, I bat my eyes at him. Before I could get stuck in a trance, I moved back.

Feeling heavy pressure on my stomach, I continued to walk down the hallway and into the arms of my mother. I was outside, I was just a kid. "Mija, didn't I tell you not to get on that swing because you were going to fall?" Lifting my chin in her hands, she planted a kiss on my forehead. Turning around to run off, I saw a black car creep up the block slowly. Looking back at my mother, I shouted. I was going to try and stand on the swing, yet again. Folding her arms across her chest, she stood there tapping her foot and looking on. Once I hopped on the swing, I pushed it slightly until I could pump my legs up and down.

Looking over to the right, the window rolled down and the shots rang out. Turning back towards my mom, she dropped to the ground with a single shot to the stomach. Before the swing could come to a full stop, I jumped off. Kids were screaming and running, while adults tried to get ahold of their children. Hitting the metal gate that was about six feet away, I fell to the ground. Jumping up, I ran to my mother who was laid out. Blood spilled from her mouth, "Mija, I love you and I love Misha." *Why the hell was she bringing up my cousin right now instead of asking for help?* "When you need help, go ask Frankie. I love you." Laying her head back, I grabbed the white tee she had on, trying to pull her up. Before I could hit her and bring her back, I was grabbed.

Gasping for air, my eyes bucked open as I tried to grab my neck.

"Relax, relax."

Looking over, my father placed his hands on my shoulders, shouting that we needed a nurse. Turning my head to the side, I looked for Asaad, I looked for Chinx, I even looked for the bastard of a fiancé of mine. Closing my eyes shut again, I wanted to go back to my dream. I wanted to see my mother again. I needed to see Asaad and ask him why Chinx grabbed me.

19

MISHA

"Asaad, I know you're kidding, right?" Sitting up in my bed looking over at the television I left on the night before. The Netflix message "are you still watching" was plastered on the screen. Wiping the cold and dry eyeliner from the corners of my eyes, I asked Assad to repeat himself.

"She got shot. Misha, listen that wasn't the plan, but it got complicated."

"Fuck you mean it got complicated? How the hell she get that deep in Asaad?" Rolling my head on my shoulders, I closed my eyes before blowing out an aspirated groan.

"Are you in the hospital with her?"

"Yeah, but I can't stay here, so call her pops and get the fuck down here quick, Misha."

"Aight." Ending the call, I dialed Oliver's number, filling him in on the details and the hospital Lou was in. He informed me he was sending me some money to catch a flight.

Jumping up from my bed, I rummaged through my drawers and closet for the first outfit I could find. Running in the bathroom, I turned on the shower. In the midst of handling my hygiene, I said a quiet prayer. I had already lost my aunt to violence; I couldn't lose Lucy. Asaad kept it short, not answering all my questions. Knowing the way the streets worked, he had something to do with her getting shot and that's why he couldn't stick around. Once I was in the tub, I let the burning hot water fall on me. Placing my head under the water, I let out a slight moan.

Washing off, I grabbed the towel that hung across the rack on my wall. Wrapping it around my body, I looked at my phone.

Asaad: if you need money to fly out there, let me know

Me: I'm good, thanks

Asaad: I'm sending you some money, anyway, make sure Lou is good.

Placing my phone back on the table, I put on my under-clothes, leggings and black tee. Picking up my small H&M crossbody purse with my wallet and keys, I reach for my phone. I looked over my shoulder for a thin sweater for the flight. After double checking for my belongings, I ordered an Uber to LaGuardia Airport. Waiting outside for the red Toyota Camry, I called Chinx, but was sent to voicemail. Smacking my lips, I figured he was going to be on some bullshit.

Letting Oliver know I was headed to the airport, he told me he had just made it to the hospital. Learning that Lou was in surgery, I was relieved to know she wasn't as bad off as I thought. Pulling into the airport, I searched for the next flight out to Raleigh. Looking down at my phone, it read three in the morning. Scanning the airport, I found the next flight that wasn't full was leaving at six in the morning. Sucking my teeth and growing impatient I bought a ticket before sitting down in one of the chairs.

Scrolling my phone to see when the last activity on Lou's social media accounts were, I needed clues or signs to see if Hassel was around. I sent Asaad a message to see if he could give me some kind of answers.

Asaad: Yo Misha, I'ma have to get back to you at a later

date. Listen, just know I'm apologizing to Lou and to you, aight?

Screwing up my face, I looked down at the message yet again. Wanting to toss my phone on the floor, I couldn't. Dialing his number over and over, he had finally answered after the fourth try.

"Why you so fucking hardheaded, Misha?"

"Well, you're not going to half ass me Asaad. What the fuck you mean you're apologizing?"

"Misha, I shouldn't have got her mixed up, but her pops is the judge. I can't do that shit."

"Not making any sense, Asaad, so you wanna try this again?"

"Misha are you fucking stupid? Listen, aight? I gotta go handle something, I'ma get back at you." With that, he hung up the phone. I was more pissed with him now than before the phone call. Yeah, I know we ain't supposed to talk over the phone, but when it comes to Lou, I needed to know it all.

Laying back in the chair, I closed my eyes until my alarm went off, letting me know it was boarding time. Checking my phone for any missed messages or calls, my mother had texted me to call her.

"Hello?"

"Girl, what the fuck you doing? Oliver's stupid ass called me and told me Lucy was shot."

"Yeah," answering her with a dry tone, I grabbed up the hoodie I brought along with my purse and boarded the plane.

"What you mean yeah? Why you ain't call me?" She sounded irritated but shit, I was pissed off not having a clear understanding of what is going on.

"Ma, I don't know much. I'm on my way over there now to see how she's doing."

"Was it that fiancé of hers? Cuz umm Oliver said that two

dudes brought her in." Rolling my eyes, the last thing I needed was for my mother to get involved in the bullshit.

"Ma listen, I'm going to board this plane. The minute I get down there, I'm going to get you updated cuz I haven't heard much." Dismissing her before she could pry any further, placing my phone on airplane mode, I took my seat.

I know Oliver better have some fucking answers for me as soon as I get there, I'm tired of the back and forth bullshit with him and Asaad.

20

OLIVER

The minute Misha called me, I hauled ass to the hospital. I wasn't about to lose my baby girl the same way I lost her mother. When Lyla was gunned down, I was working and received the call a little too late. Stepping foot in the familiar hospital, my stomach jumped with anxiety. This was the same hospital Lyla was pronounced dead in.

Making my way to the front desk, the security guard stopped me. Tapping my shoulder, he told me she was rushed in with the paramedics, but he did see a car drive off with a guy inside. Stopping short, I ran my hand over my head before calling Hassel. Pacing back and forth, his phone rang out until the voicemail picked up. Dialing his mother's number, she answered.

"They killed my boy and I know your stupid ass daughter had something to do with it, Oliver!" Snapping my neck back, I took the phone away from my ear, looking down at it before placing it back to my ear.

"Bitch, my daughter is laid up in the hospital fighting for her life now, the fuck is you talking about?" Snapping out of character, I had to remind myself that I was in the hospital and I was the judge of the state.

"Oh, fighting for her life?" she asked like she was surprised.

"Yeah, she got shot, so where the fuck was your son shot, cuz I need answers."

"I'm not sure because he was clearly brought to my house and dumped on the street like an animal."

Shaking my head, I thought *he was an animal*. He was buying drugs and selling them to the neighborhood. How ironic the nigga was the pastor who was well connected to know who was who?

"I get that, well who wanted him dead?"

I knew the niggas in the hospital wanted him dead, shit they made it very evident, but I also knew that I recognized a name on the paper who would also want him dead. I have yet to put the pieces together, but I will.

"Them fucking New York dudes, probably the same mutha-fuckas who killed June."

"Aight listen, I ain't got time for speculations. I gotta go see about my daughter." Ending the call, I was taken to her room. Standing in the doorway from afar, I looked at her.

The minute she started stirring in the bed, I ran to her side. Placing my hands on her shoulders, Lucy was panicking. Trying to calm her down, I reached over to press the button alerting the nurses. "Lucy calm down." She looked around trying to lift herself up off the bed.

"Where is everyone?" The way she asked me was as if she knew someone else was supposed to be there.

"Who? Baby, who shot you?" Pulling up a chair beside her bed, sitting down, I looked her in her eyes. "Tell me something."

"I want to go to New York, where is Misha?"

The nurses rushed into the room. Scooting the chair back, I allowed them to check her out. Checking her vitals and asking a bunch of questions regarding her health, the officers looked into the room. Waving in my direction, I followed them into the hallway.

"We found the body of the pastor, so it looks like they were targeted." Giving him a half eye roll, I wanted to respond *no shit muthafucka* but I allowed him to keep talking. "We hope she can ID the guys and I say guys because Hassel was shot with two different guns."

Sighing heavily, I comb my fingers through my salt and pepper beard. "Well, she only asked where her cousin was."

"Okay, well can we go in and talk to her?"

Gesturing for them to go in the room, they waited for the nurses to leave.

21

LOU

I knew these two fucking cops was going to start with their bullshit the minute they walked in the room. If they thought I was about to sell out Asaad and Chinx they had another thing coming. One thing my mother always told me was to never snitch, karma would come back ten times worse. Looking past them, I shook my head at my father, who clearly didn't budge. Rolling my head on my shoulder, I reached for the cup of water on the table.

"Lucy, I hope you can help us catch he the guys who did this to you and a Hassel."

"What did they do to Hassel?" I mean, I knew they shot him but shit the nigga survived the last shooting he was mixed up in like he had nine lives or something.

"He was murdered and found in front of his mother's house." My eyes widened with shock, I figured Asaad and Chinx were ruthless, but I ain't expect them to be this fucking sick. *Yeah, that bastard had some questions to answer,* I thought looking back at the cop.

"No, I honestly don't know who was after us, I mean besides the crew he had been around lately, I'm not sure." Putting on my best award winning Oscar performance, I forced the tears out of my eyes. Giving it my all, I sniffed choking back. Lifting my hand to my nose, I shook my head slowly. "I need to see my fiancé." If looks could kill, I'm sure my father would be strangling the life out of me right now. *Oh fucking well, I'm tired of these niggas,* I thought.

"Okay Lucy, we're sorry. I'm sure we can get you that information to go and see your fiancé." Digging into his pocket, he removed a card. "If you happen to remember anything or something pops up, just give us a call, please."

Nodding my head in agreeance, I took the card from his hand. Sliding it on the table by the bed, I watched them leave out.

"I'm not them naive sheriffs, so get to talking Lucy!" My father grabbed the chair with one hand, sitting in it. Cocking his legs open, he cracked his knuckles like he always did when he was serious. Looking away to avoid eye contact, he reached over and popped my hand. "What the fuck happened?"

"Daddy, I don't know. Damn, did you not hear me tell the officers that?"

"Don't fucking play with me little girl, you done scared me and Misha."

Laying back on the bed I held onto my stomach. The painkillers they gave me were starting to wear off and he was now giving me a headache.

"Listen, I know you know I'm not playing; you better be telling me every fucking thing."

"Oh, like you been telling me every fucking thing?" Shaking my head from side to side for emphasis on how he was moving, I continued, "I saw you looking on the paper that I showed you with the names of the guys in my house, so you mind telling me which muthafucka you know?"

Any other time I wouldn't be talking to him with so much aggression, but I was tired of him thinking he could run my life.

Looking down at my phone, I saw a message from Misha telling me that my father said he had to talk to the both of us together. Giving him the okie dokie look, and rolling my eyes, I continued badgering him. "So you wanna tell me something or cat got your tongue?"

"Lucy, don't play with me. You're lucky we're in this hospital or I'd knock your smart ass out."

"No, you're lucky I'm in this hospital or I'd be far away from your fraud ass."

"I've had enough of you talking out the side of your mouth," jumping up from the chair, he leaned in my direction. On impulse, I moved back to avoid getting popped by him.

"Am I disturbing anything?" Turning on his heels, I looked around him watching Misha enter the room. Silently thanking god, I flashed a fake smile in her direction.

"You know what, I'm out of here. I'll be back Lucy, and when I come back you better have some fucking answers for me."

"Or what? Cuz I already told you like I told them, I don't know who shot me, but since you're so popular, why not put your ear to the streets and see who did and where my fiancé's body is." Breathing heavily, he looked over at me then, looked at Misha who shrugged at him.

When he was out of the door, I asked Misha if she had heard anything from Asaad. She showed me the messages from the conversation they had earlier. Noticing my phone was on ten percent, I took her phone and called him. Assad dodged a few calls before finally picking up.

"Asaad is this what you're doing?" Trying to keep my voice low, Misha made herself comfortable in the chair.

"Lou listen, ya state is hot right now, and I can't afford to get caught up."

"What the hell you mean get caught up?" Smacking my lips, I couldn't believe this nigga.

"Lou, do you not know who your father is? Them niggas know you and him, so I can't get caught slipping."

"So, just like that, huh? You just up and leave me like that? So, this shit must have only meant something to me, right?" Feeling my voice crack, I looked away from Misha.

"Lou, at the end of the day, I'm married and you were engaged."

"Say less, that's the New York term, right?" Ending the call before he could say another word, I handed the phone to her. "Misha, keep that bastard away from me. He shot me and he can't even be a man and face me!" The tears that I fought to keep in spilled from my eyes and down my cheek.

"How did he shoot you Lou?" Looking over her shoulder, she lowered her voice. "Was Hassel with you?"

"Yeah, Asaad made me lure him to us and instead of going back in the hotel, Chinx used me as bait to make it look good." Shaking my head, I told her to drop the conversation. "I need to get out of here, though. I'm not staying down here with my father, Misha."

"I understand, you can come stay with me or mama."

"Yeah." For the first time in a long time, I felt a spark with a nigga that I thought I would never feel again and he played me. *He's married. So married that his finger was in my pussy in a public bathroom, huh,* I thought brushing it off.

"Listen fuck him, we only cool cuz his pops know my mom and they go way back." Shrugging her shoulders, she tapped her foot. "He's a dog ass nigga anyway. He married yet running behind you."

"Whose his father?" With a look of concern on my face, I waited for Misha to answer even though I knew none of them New York guys since I was not allowed up there.

"Some dude named Frankie; you probably don't know him

though." Misha got up, asking if I wanted any food, I was starving but the food wasn't even on my mind. I knew my father had gasped at a name on that paper I took a picture of and thinking on it, the name Frankie was at the top of the list. What Hassel had got caught up with was starting to make sense. This nigga was really knee deep in the game and my ass was so wrapped around my perfect little world that I hadn't even noticed.

I should have started questioning shit when he proposed with this expensive ass rock or the car he bought me a few weeks after. But no I was just happy my dude was legit and could spoil me. Removing the ring I stashed it in the small purse I had. Wanting to have one up on my homegirl Jen, *shit I hadn't even reached out to her.* Bringing myself back to reality I grabbed my phone forgetting it was dead. Getting Misha to leave her phone with me while she went to get some food, I called Jen. Her ass was with a petty hustler so I know she was up this early in the morning.

"Hello?" she asked in a groggy tone.

"Jen it's Lou, can you get up and talk?"

"First of all bitch, where the fuck you been? And second, yes I can get up and talk because you got a lot of explaining to do." Sounding as if she had sat up in bed, I heard her dude Truce ask her if she was good. "Yea baby, I'm talking to Lou's crazy ass."

"Listen, I know I been acting funky lately but I'm at the hospital. You wanna swing by and I tell you this shit in person?"

"Yeah, I'll be there, wait why the hell you in the hospital?"

"Jen just get here, hurry the hell up and bring your charger."

"Aight."

～

20 MINUTES LATER...

JEN WAS RUSHING into the room while me and Misha were sitting on my bed looking at SVU. Looking up at the door, I saw the panicked look on her face. Cracking a smile, she came to my side pulling me into her embrace and holding on.

"Hoe, you choking me, damn."

"Well I feel like I ain't seen ya ass in forever, you go missing after the shootout in the house then I find out Hassel was gunned down and the next thing I know they reported your ass was shot too."

"Yea," raising my brows I looked over at Misha. "Y'all know each other, right?" They both nodded in agreement. "Anyway yea all that shit happened but I can't tell you much cuz I really don't know too much." Jen gave me a look of me trying to feed her bullshit.

"I didn't just become your best friend and I know Hassel is deeper in the shit then you think cuz Truce said he was hearing his name around."

"Well, he apparently owed someone and... well, they came to finish the job; I just so happened to be in the wrong place at the wrong fucking time." Sighing, I fell back on the bed looking up at the ceiling in the hospital room. "This nigga really was dealing though Jen and I'm not talking 'bout no weed."

"Bitch I know, I told you Truce heard his name around." Laughing she looked up at me, "You good though, right?"

"Yeah, I'm good but Jen, I'm not staying here. The minute I'm good to go, which is hopefully tomorrow, I'm going back to New York."

"Why?"

"My father is really irking my nerves and now that Hassel is gone, I don't want to be down here around his enemies."

"Well bitch I heard his enemies is from New York, his

mother was on the news talking about the niggas was the same niggas who pretty much killed Mr. June."

Screwing up my face, I could have sworn the news reported Mr. June's murder as a senseless drive by shooting, so I ain't know what the hell Jen was talking about. Jen pulled out her phone and went to the news reporting, and damn right Henrietta's ol' messy ass was on their naming the shooters as people from New York. Putting the pieces together, she said her son was mixed-up trying to help some guys get out of trouble and that's where they got him involved. Rolling my eyes I looked at her put on her best performance just like I had done a few hours earlier.

Henrietta then goes on to tell people I was shot as well and she had yet to find out the status on me. *Bitch won't find out either. Hmm, maybe I should keep up her fucking lie,* I thought just as my phone began vibrating, looking down I saw "Mother in law" flash across the screen.

"Hello." I placed the phone on speaker for the girls to hear.

"Oh my god! Thank god you're okay, baby! Is it okay if I come and see you?"

"Sure, I'm still a little woozy but I don't think that should be a problem." Lying through my teeth, I didn't want her to think I was up all this time.

"Okay, what hospital are you in?"

"Wake Med Raleigh Campus." Ending the call, I sat back waiting on the drama queen to arrive.

22

———

ASAAD

The flight back to New York was draining, the whole trip to North Carolina was draining, but I was happy the nigga Hassel was handled. He was doing shit way too dirty out here, and from the looks of things, everyone was shocked he was running the streets anyway. I was pissed off that Lou got hit in the process, but that muthafucka caught me off guard. I knew shutting her out was going to kill me and her, but I needed to get far away from her. With her father being mixed up in the law, I couldn't risk getting caught for anyone.

Pulling up to my house, I saw countless items that belonged to me stacked up in the front yard, standing there in amazement, I ran my fingers through my beard. "This looney bitch better not be here or I'ma fuck her up!" Mumbling, I jogged up the driveway and I inserted my key. Pushing open the door, the smell of ammonia and bleach filled my nostrils. Placing my hand over my nose, I walked through the house. Clothing and shoes were scattered all over the living room floor, staining the rugs. Calling out to Gabby, I waited to hear her shout something stupid, but the house was silent. Walking through to where she stayed at, it was empty. Taking pictures of what had happened, I headed straight to the lawyer. Sitting in the waiting area, I pulled out my phone scrolling to where Lou's name was. Typing up a message, I read it over before backspacing and deleting it entirely.

I couldn't go down that route with her, she was surrounded by toxicity yet she was so peaceful. Lou has a little fire in her but anybody could see looking into her almond-shaped eyes that she was just as soft as they came. Her lips were soft, her hands were soft and those curls she loved to rock were soft too. Hearing my name called, I popped up. After following behind the lawyer, I got straight to it.

"I want to file for divorce." Looking up from her desk, she side eyed me. Her long wavy weave was pulled to the back, behind her ears with a part down the middle. The black dress she wore was a size too small to be a lawyer, but who was I to judge?

"So, Mr. Daniels is this your choice, or will your wife be storming in here soon?" Staring in my eyes, she licked her plump lips.

"Nah, she wants to be together, but I ain't feelin' it so...." Sitting back in the cherry oak chair in front of her, I continued, "Check this out, we were only staying together because our house value will be more in a few months, but the bitch," raising her brows in my direction, I stopped short, "my bad, the *crazy chick* done trashed all my clothes and shoes. So, before I hurt her, I need to walk away." Pulling out my phone, she leaned back in the chair before picking up the coffee cup off the table. Taking a sip, I searched through my videos, until I came across what I was looking for.

Handing her the phone, she brushed her manicured fingers across my hand. If I ain't know better, I'd say the bitch was flirting with me. Pointing to the phone, she looked down at Gabby acting a fool on social media. Shaking her head, she looked back up at me.

"Ms. Waters listen, I don't even need shit; I just need to get the hell on and take my name back."

"You got another woman?" Not understanding why that was her business, I told her no. She ain't need to know about Lou, shit, I don't even know if I know about her. I'm sure Lou was done with my ass after I told her to bounce.

"Okay, cool. I'll need you to fill out some work and then we can get this process started."

"Aight, say less." Grabbing up a pen, I went and filled out the paperwork. An hour later and the divorce was filed. Standing up and stretching my arms, I noticed Ms. Waters stealing glances down at my pants. Making sure to give her something to look at, I made a mental note to wear jeans if I had to come back to this office. Stepping out of the office, my phone was ringing. Looking down at the name flash on the screen, I picked up.

"Sup."

"Don't answer the phone all nonchalant, why the fuck you left his bitch alive?"

"Pops c'mon now, she ain't gonna say shit."

"And you know that how? Bitches will give up a nigga in a heartbeat. I keep telling your ass that!" he barked into the line, dismissing the idea of telling him that Lou wasn't that type; then I'd have to go and explain everything.

"Pops, can you trust me on this?" Walking to the car I hopped in, letting it warm up. I placed my phone on the holder.

"Yeah, I trust you, but I don't trust no bitch!" The hatred that dropped from his voice told me there was more to his trust issues, but I wasn't about to pry further.

"Aight, well I got it handled." Adjusting my seat, I leaned it back, getting comfortable.

"You got my bread? I need to link up with you and Chinx in a few."

"No doubt, say less." Ending the call, I pulled up Misha's

number. I know I told Lou all that shit, but I needed to check on her. Sending her a message, she responded in a few seconds.

Misha: fuck off Asaad, you hurt my cousin.

Asaad: **Mish c'mon, tell her it ain't like that.**

Misha: **Nigga you mentioned you was married to her, fuck you thought?**

Asaad: **I need to see her. Get her here ASAP.**

Misha: **No.**

Grabbing my phone off the holder, I dialed her number. The fuck she mean no? All the shit I did for Misha in the past; she owed me this solid.

"What?"

"Relax with all that what bullshit, where is she? Let me speak to her Misha."

"No, she doesn't want to speak to you, hence the reason she blocked your number!"

"Misha, you fucking owe me! I done saved your dumb ass on many occasions from Don." I wasn't the type to throw up the shit I did, but today Misha had me fucked up. "So you gonna put that word in or what? Cuz I'm tired of going back and forth with your ass."

"Whatever yo, you did that shit cuz you wanted to, and I don't want to do this so." Hanging up in my ear, I hit the steering wheel with force, setting off the horn. Dialing Lou's number, I saw Misha was right. She had blocked me, but I needed to get her to me before my father put a hit out on her.

Sending Misha a text, I apologized for the shit, but I needed to get in touch with Lou. It was important.

Driving off, I ended up at the bar, ordering a double shot of Hennessy. I let the cognac slide down my throat smoothly. Raising the shot glass, I told them give me another two. Shit was going downhill. Instead of falling back from the game here, I was getting deeper than I should. The woman I was married to was a piece of work and the woman I was lusting over wanted nothing to do with me since I shot her. Feeling the vibration in my phone, I grabbed it up and put it on airplane mode. Six shots later, I was stumbling to the parking lot. Walking right into my father, he grabbed up my six foot frame as if I was the cowardly little boy from back in the days.

"The fuck is wrong with your drunk ass? Get him in the fucking car!" Tapping my pockets, he found my car keys. His two men tossed me in the backseat of my car, hitting my head on the door.

"Fuck!" Running my hand over my head, my father sucked his teeth.

"Shut the fuck up pussy." Hopping in the driver's seat, he pulled off in the direction of his house.

"Shit, I'm fucked up."

23

LOU

A week later and I was finally leaving the damn hospital. Between my father coming in and out of here and Henrietta harassing me, I was over this damn state. Misha let me know I could stay at her place until I got on my feet, but that wasn't something I wanted to do. She lived in a small two bedroom with two bad ass kids. I was used to my space, so that would be an adjustment I couldn't take.

Henrietta had the funeral scheduled for tonight, and although I didn't want to go, I knew I had no choice but to show my face. I mean he was a dude I had loved until he began changing up on me. Once I was in the house, I had an eerie feeling wash over me. Misha must have sensed my hesitation. Looking over to me, she saw the residue from the yellow tape left behind.

"Why didn't they clean up all this shit?" Ripping down the small amount of tape on the wall near the stairs, she told me to go sit down. Shaking off the feeling, I told her I wanted to just grab some clothes and bounce. Walking up the stairs to the bedroom, the carpet was removed, looking down the hallway to where Hassel's office was, I sighed heavily, thinking about the shooting. I swore I was over it. I thought I wouldn't feel anything, but I was wrong.

Entering the room I headed to the closet trying to hold back my tears. I was really crying and I didn't want to. I really was leaving this shit behind, the last three years of my life, the nigga I thought I wanted to marry and have his kids set me up for failure. Grabbing as much clothing off the hangers as possible, I stuffed it in my suitcases. Three suitcases later filled with clothing and shoes; I was leaving out of the house I had made my home.

"You ready?" Misha asked me, pulling one of the suitcases. Ordering an Uber to Jen's house, I told her I had no choice. When the gray Toyota Camry pulled up, I got in. The drive was silent, just the way I wanted. Looking out of the window, I was so ready to get my ass far away from here.

24

MISHA

ooking over at Lou, I knew she was really hurting. She could front for everyone else like she was truly over this shit, but if the nigga I was engaged to told everyone I was the one mixed-up in this shit, I'd be hurt too. I was pissed that she had to even come to this fucking funeral to begin with. The nigga didn't give a fuck about her. His mother was an overbearing asshole and her father wanted to grill her about who shot her every few minutes.

I didn't want to be at this funeral myself, but I came because Jen offered to drive us to the airport once this thing is over with. The more I stayed around these people, the more I caught myself drinking. Shit, if Lou downed one more shot, I was going to scream for them to get the fuck from around her. Walking into the church, Lou looked uneasy, her father was sitting right in the front, waving for her to come over. Sucking my teeth, I followed her there, grabbing her arm before we reached him, I whispered, asking if she was good. Lou nodded and we proceeded to sit down.

Two hours and a million speakers later, I was ready for them to close the fucking casket. We were already sitting in the front row and Lou was having mini breakdowns every so often. Her father kept squeezing her arm as if she was a damn kid. The minute they asked her to speak Lou got up and walked out. Following behind her, she told me she couldn't be there anymore. That was magic to my fucking ears, pulling out her phone before I could get in touch with Jen, she was making her way out the door.

"I'm done with this shit," Lou whispered to the both of us, causing us to laugh. Before we could walk off, Oliver was shouting her name. Rolling my eyes in my head she turned around and asked, "What?"

"You leaving and you won't even say bye to me."

"Cuz I rather not say bye to you, I would rather just leave."

"Lucy get over here now!" Stomping off in his direction, me and Jen looked on. He gave her a tight hug and let her go, Lucy ran from him so fast to the car, I had to keep up.

"Girl wait up, the hell is your problem?"

"How about you go ask that damn asshole what my problem is?"

Turning on my heels, I marched over to Oliver who was standing on the grass looking stupid. "What did you say to her?"

"Listen aight, don't come over here on the bullshit Misha, I was talking to my daughter. Why not go ask your so called mother."

"Excuse me, my so called mother?" I asked, furrowing my brows in his direction.

Lou stepped out the car and yelled, "Misha fuck him!"

"Little girl, you got one more time to disrespect the lord!" Oliver yelled back at Lou who was holding onto the passenger door.

"Like you ain't been disrespecting the lord lying? You stupid son of a bitch!" My eyes widened in shock as I hauled ass to the car. Pushing Lou in, I was not about to witness her damn murder today. When the doors were closed, Oliver tapped on the hood of the car. Telling Jen to drive off. Lou insisted she stay there.

"Lou I'm not up for this today. Let's just go, okay?"

"No, you need to stop acting like a punk Misha. That man told me that you're my sister but he's not your father."

"What?"

"Exactly, so what you trying to do?"

"Jen just drive off; I need to go talk to my mother." Falling back against the backseat, I lifted my phone and started texting my mother nonstop about the bomb that was dropped on me.

25

ASAAD

Sitting in the rent office going over some paperwork, I was stressed out. After getting the third degree from my father, I told him I filed for divorce. He told me Gabby was going to flip out. Not giving a fuck, I told him it was what it was. I was cool with that shit until she finally got wind of the divorce filing. She been blowing up my phone, dogging me on social media and popping up at my damn office. Staying in a hotel to avoid her was the stupidest shit I had to do.

Hearing talking from outside, I looked up spotting Misha and Lou walking by. Dropping the paper in my hand, I jumped up from my desk. Fixing my shirt and rubbing my hand through my hair, I needed to get next to Lou, I didn't give a fuck how thirsty I was. Opening the door, I yelled out to her. She turned her head, bouncing her curls on her shoulder. She looked at me and rolled her eyes. Turning back around, she dragged the suitcases in her hands.

Jogging up behind her, I took one of the suitcases from her hands. "Misha wassup? Lou, let me holla at you really quick."

"No, Assad she's busy."

"Misha, with all due respect I'm talking to her."

"And I'm telling you no—" before she could finish going off on me, Lou turned to her and told Misha she was only going to be a few minutes. Walking them the rest of the way, Misha had an attitude, sucking her teeth and sighing over and over. I was relieved when we reached her apartment. Misha and Lou disappeared inside before Lou came back out alone.

Looking down at the cracked concrete, she twirled her fingers together. Just as I've always done, I grabbed her chin and told her to look at me. "Lou come hear me out. I ain't trying to do this shit in the streets."

"You shot me Asaad and left me," her voice cracked as she whispered what I did to her. I knew what the hell I did, I ain't perfect, but I wasn't going to let her keep throwing it up in my face. Grabbing her hand, I dragged her to my office. Once we were inside, I closed the door.

"Lou, I know what I did. I fucked up, aight?"

"So, what do you want Asaad? For me to accept that shit?" Snapping her neck and smacking her lips, she leaned against the door, folding her arms across her chest. She had on a V-neck shirt that stopped just at her cleavage, showing off just the right amount. The high waist jeans she had on accentuated her hips, driving me crazy. My dick jumped as she licked her plump lips.

"Lou, I want you to come let me love you."

"Nigga are you crazy? You're fucking married, remember?" Turning to leave out, I grabbed her by her waist, pulling her back. When her ass pressed against my dick, I leaned into her neck, kissing her. Lou let out a slight moan, laying her head back. Playing with her zipper, she told me to stop. Trying to break free of my grasp.

"Lou listen, I filed for divorce. That shit is dead; it's been dead."

"Wasn't that dead when I was laid up in the hospital. Do you know I got everyone believing I don't know who fucking shot me Asaad!" Turning her towards me, Lou had tears rolling down her face. *Shit I hated to see her cry,* I thought, wiping her tears. Pulling her into my chest, Lou broke down. That shit killed me knowing I was the cause of it.

Banging on my office door brought us back to reality. She backed away, wiping her eyes, furrowing her brows. "Who is that?" Shrugging my shoulders, I moved her behind me. When I pulled open the door, Gabby stood there with her fist up ready to bang on the door again.

"What the fuck is your problem Gabriella?" Using her full name, she cocked her head to the side pushing past me. Lou stood on the opposite side of the room annoyed.

"So, this is why you're filing for divorce cuz you fucking with one of these hood rat bitches!"

Lou started laughing, only pissing Gabby off more, "Bitch I know you're not laughing. I will come fuck you up."

"You can try." Brushing her off, Lou walked around her, "Assad, when you handle this then reach out to me." Stepping out of the office, I shook my head before grabbing Gabby by the arm. This wasn't a fight she wanted to have, especially since Lou wasn't alone.

Slamming the door shut, I looked at Gabby, "Yo you know what this is, your ass bleached my shit after I left out to handle business!"

"Asaad I was drunk and pissed off, I'm sorry." Gabby's fake ass apology only pissed me off further.

"Gabby fuck all the bullshit, you always drunk and always spending my money."

"You never complained before, now all of a sudden it's a problem?" Balling up her fist, I warned her if she hit me, I was going to fuck her up. "Do you love her?"

"If I say no, will you take your crazy ass outta here?"

"Fuck you Asaad, she must have let you fuck already." Hunching her shoulders over, she turned, "I'm not giving you a divorce, so you better tell that bitch you're still married!" The minute she stormed out of the office; I slammed my door shut. Running to my desk to grab my phone, I scrolled to Lou's name.

"So, I'm guessing ya wife is gone?"

"Yeah, she's gone Lou. Come have lunch with me."

"You asking or you telling?" Hearing the sarcasm in her voice only made me want to get her close to me.

"I'm telling you, so meet me in the parking lot in ten minutes." Being straight forward, I was tired of playing around with her.

"Asaad, I'm busy, and it would take me longer than ten minutes."

"Lou, I said ten minutes, so you better make a miracle happen before I come banging on Misha's door."

Ending the call, I headed to the car, leaning up on the door, I looked on at the kids playing in the park. It was late afternoon and I already wanted to go get a drink, pulling a half smoked blunt out my back pocket, I lit it, inhaling the smoke thinking about the shit I was dealing with. Gabby was making this divorce harder than I needed, Lou definitely wasn't going to deal with me knowing I was still married to her crazy ass.

"You give me ten minutes so you can smoke a blunt?" Rolling her eyes, Lou walked around me to the passenger side of the car.

"Shit, I ain't think your ass was coming." Turning around, I opened the car door.

"You're not even a gentleman, you can't even open the door for me, but want me to go to lunch with you." Hopping in the car, Lou slammed the door shut.

"My bad, you caught me off guard."

"Umm hmm," was all she said before putting her seatbelt on.

26

LOU

Sitting in the car, Asaad scrolled through his phone, I guess searching for a song to play. Turning my head towards the window, I rolled it down. The stench of weed was overwhelming and I didn't want it stuck on my clothing. Closing my eyes and laying my head back, I felt his hand rest on my thigh. Popping my eyes open I looked over at him. His eyes were red and low. "You look stressed out."

"I am, that's why I'm trying to get close to you, you don't stress me."

"You ain't bringing that toxic shit around me Asaad, you know what I just went through."

"I know Lou, come go away with me." Looking at him in annoyance I had to ask him was he serious. He shook his head yes. Rolling my eyes I popped his hand.

"Don't touch me nigga, you on some bullshit and you think I'm stupid!"

"Lou what the fuck you talking about? I'm trying to get to know you."

"So why you can't get to know me here? Why we gotta go away?" Smacking my lips, I asked, "What did your wife say?"

"She said I hope that hoe got some good pussy. I told her I haven't felt it yet but it tastes amazing!" Playfully punching him on the arm, he laughed in my face, "On the real Lou, come away with me. I'm sure we both can use it."

Laying my head back, thinking about being on somebody's island, away from everything did sound relaxing, but at what cost? "Just drive and take me to lunch, Asaad."

"Aight, I can do that." Starting up the car and driving off, he kept his right hand rested on my thigh. Closing my eyes again, I dozed off until Asaad's lips brushed against mine. Jumping up from my sleep, he was staring in my face.

"What type of creep shit you on?"

"You're beautiful."

"Whatever." Looking around, I tried to see if I knew where I was. Seeing the name of the hotel, I sucked my teeth. "So, you bring me to a hotel, Asaad? You not getting no pussy."

"I brought you here cuz they have a great chef and this is where my ass been staying until I can get me a spot."

"I guess." Following behind him, I grabbed a hold of his hand. Walking and looking around, we got on the elevator and headed up to the twentieth floor. Once we got in the room, I told him I wanted to take a shower and get comfortable.

"You good, I'ma go and get some shit from the store."

"Okay." Watching him leave out of the room, I turned on my heels and headed to the bathroom. For him to be a man he was neat; a little too neat if you ask me, but I wasn't complaining. Pulling back the curtains, I turned on the water to the jacuzzi tub. Turning off the water, I opted for taking a shower instead of a bat. I was horny and Asaad's sexy ass wasn't making it any better by touching on me and roaming my body with his eyes. Removing my clothes, I dropped them on the floor. Stepping into the hot water, I unraveled the hair scrunchie on my curls. Allowing the water to fall on me, I washed up. Fifteen minutes later, I was stepping out of the tub with my curls drenched and my body cold. Drying off, I grabbed the extra robe that hung behind the door in the bathroom.

Opening the door I stuck my head out and realized Asaad still wasn't there. Hoping that he stayed out for longer than I anticipated, I walked over to the bed. Untying the robe, I laid across the bed. Spreading my legs, I thought about Asaad. I wanted his dick in my mouth. I wanted to feel him. Licking my lips, my hands cupped my breasts massaging my nipples. Letting out a slight moan, I opened my mouth, rolling my eyes in the back of my head. Using my right hand, I ran it down my stomach to my pussy. Massaging my clit slowly, my legs fell to the side. With my left hand squeezing my breast, I bit on my bottom lip.

"Shit!" inserting my middle finger inside of my pussy, I gyrated my hips to my own beat. Imagining Asaad fucking my face, I finger fucked myself. Feeling my juices coat my finger, the sound of the door unlocking only heightened my arousal.

"Hmm, shit!" Massaging myself with one hand and fingering myself with my other, I looked on at Asaad as he stood there. Dropping the bag he had on the table.

"Damn Lou, can I watch?" Nodding to him, he pulled up a chair at the table, sitting in front of me.

"Asaad, I want to fuck you; I want to suck your dick!" Looking at me, he bit his bottom lip. Leaning back in the chair, Asaad took out his dick jerking it. Getting up, I crawled over to him on my knees, with lust in my eyes.

Taking him in my mouth, he moaned in pleasure, "Shit Lou." Using my hands to jerk him off, I continued to bob my head up and down on his dick.

Grabbing my curls in his hand, he guided my head up and down the shaft of his dick. Gagging, I took all of him in my mouth.

"Fuck!" The sound of him enjoying this turned me on more. Removing him from my mouth, I slapped his dick on my face, licking the tip and sucking it. Licking the shaft, I massaged his balls.

"Nah, Lou, I'm 'bout to bust, get up!" Continuing to suck and lick on his dick, the precum slid down my throat. Asaad gripped my hair just as the cum shot down my throat, "Fuck!" Getting up off my knees, I head to the bathroom to clean out my mouth. Looking in the mirror feeling good about myself, there was a knock on the door.

"Lou, nah you ain't right!" Laughing to myself, I used the washcloth to wipe my face after rinsing my mouth.

Stepping out of the bathroom, Asaad was sitting in the chair with his boxers and a tank on. His arms and chest were cut up. Taking the bottle out of the bag, he set it on the floor.

"You good Asaad?"

"Nah, come sit that pussy on me and then I'll be good." Batting my lashes in his face, he got up, letting me know he was going to shower before we ate food. Agreeing, I climbed in the bed, got under the blanket and dozed off. Waking up to Asaad spreading my legs apart, trailing kisses up my thighs, he lifted my right leg. Looking down at him, he winked, sending a chill through my body.

"Asaad don't take your time, it's been so long since I've felt a stiff dick!" Cupping his mouth over my pussy, I stopped mid-sentence, squirming in his hands. Lapping his tongue over my clit sent me over the edge. Backing away, Asaad held onto my hips with his hands. Unable to move, he inserted his finger, sucking slowly on my swollen clit. Getting up, he allowed the towel to fall. Looking down at his stiff dick, I wanted to back down, but the way my juices ran down his hand, I knew I needed this. Using his dick, he rubbed it against my folds. Spreading my lips apart, he placed the tip inside of me. Raising my legs, I gasped with excitement, "Damn, your pussy tight, Lou!"

Looking around the room, he backed out of me. Getting up on my arms, I asked him what he was doing.

"I need a condom."

"Asaad, if you don't come and fuck me right now, I will leave." Walking back over to the bed, Asaad lifted me up, pulling me down on his erect dick. I relaxed, taking all of him. The pain subsided, bouncing up and down on his dick, he bit his bottom lip. Throwing my head back, Asaad cupped my right breast, sucking on my nipple. Heightening my excitement, I told him I was cumming. Lifting me up, I got on all fours. Entering me from the back, Asaad grabbed a handful of my hair. Screaming out in ecstasy, I said, "Asaad shit, fuck me!" Trying to match his rhythm, I closed my eyes as a single tear fell.

Slapping my ass, he moaned and groaned. "This my pussy, Lou?" Knowing it was his now, I nodded my head. "I asked is this my pussy?"

"Yes, Asaad." Speaking in tongues, I came hard. Feeling my body jerking, Asaad laid me flat on the bed, trying not to put pressure on my stomach, fucking me slow, then spread my buttchecks. Laying there trying to catch my breath, Asaad moaned he was cumming. Shooting up inside of me, he slowed down his pace. Looking over my shoulder, my eyes were low, staring at Asaad pull out of me. I rolled over to my back. He disappeared into the bathroom, returning with a warm rag. "I'ma go shower, if you want to join me c'mon." Sliding off the bed, my legs were regaining strength, pulling back the shower curtain, I reached into the shower. Asaad walked up behind me playfully slapping my ass.

"Don't start."

"Why not? I can finish that shit."

Looking back at him, I smirked, "I'm sure I'll put you to bed."

"Yeah, aight." Stepping in the shower, Asaad followed

behind me. "You staying with me or you going back to Misha's crib?"

"Whatever works for you baby." The sound of his phone interrupted our conversation. Letting it ring out to voicemail, his phone began ringing again. Sucking his teeth, I told him go answer it.

"Nah, it's probably Gabby's crazy ass." Cocking my head to the side, his phone went off again.

"Asaad, go answer it, damn." Watching him leave out the bathroom, I washed off trying to ignore his call.

27

ASAAD

"**P**ops, I hope it's an emergency the way you keep blowing me up."

"Nigga, if you see me blowing you the fuck up, why your ass ain't answering?" Hearing him grunt into the line, he said, "Let me guess, you in there fucking that girl, huh?"

"What? Listen pops, don't call me on no bullshit that Gabby probably running to tell you."

"Oh, trust I'm not believing no woman scorned, I asked Chinx what the fuck happened in North Carolina and well, now I know some shit."

"Fuck you talking 'bout?" Furrowing my brows, I heard Lou behind me. Turning in her direction, I placed my finger over my lips to keep her quiet. Her hair was dripping wet and the robe was swallowing her petite frame. *Damn she was fucking gorgeous.*

"Get the fuck over here Asaad." Ending the call, I told Lou I had to run out and handle some business. The pout on her face told me she wanted to put up a fight but decided against it.

"You coming back here or should I go back to Misha's house?"

"I want you here when I get back Lou, eat the food and chill out." Throwing on a sweat suit, I grabbed my nine out the nightstand. Lou looked away, she hated when I ran the streets, but she knew this is who I was.

"Be safe." Standing on her tiptoes, she kissed me on my lips. Picking her up, I pinned her to the wall.

"You gonna be here when I get back?"

"Yes Saad, just don't have me waiting forever." Putting her down, I grabbed my keys and phone, leaving out the room. Racing to my car, I texted Chinx to see what all he told my pops about Lou, when he didn't respond in a few minutes, I called him.

"Yerr."

"Nah nigga, what you told my pops about Lou?"

Clearing his throat, "I ain't say too much but that she was Hassel's ex."

"Nigga, what the fuck? Now you really thought my pops was going to be cool with that shit?"

"Listen, the nigga ain't no saint, so why you trippin'?"

"Just keep the shit you find out between me and you, the less he knows the better." Hopping in my car, I started it up, driving straight to Kew Gardens where my father owned a townhouse. Listening to Nipsey Hussle's "Dedication," I ran the track back three times before pulling up to the driveway. It was a Thursday, so I knew my mother was in the kitchen cooking up dinner. Jumping out of the car, I noticed Chinx's ride parked up the block. Grabbing my sweats up over my ass, I tapped on the front door. My pops opened the door with a lit blunt in his hand, his salt and pepper hair was trimmed low on his head. He sported a goatee displaying the freckles on his cheeks. Stepping aside, I walked in. Smelling the fried chicken, my stomach grumbled. Hadn't been able to eat in the hotel since Lou had other plans, and I was starving.

"Took your ass long enough," my father said, turning in the

opposite direction towards the living room. Stepping into the kitchen, I placed a kiss on my mother's cheek. She was much shorter than I was, standing at five-feet three-inches. Her wavy, jet-black hair was brushed to the back of her head. Her smooth, cocoa complexion was piled with her favorite coconut oil, giving it a glow.

"Hey baby."

Back in the days, I knew my mother turned many heads, in her early fifties she still had it going on. Sharee wasn't your petite kind of woman, she was a curvy woman. I'm pretty sure that's what drew my father to her.

"You good?" I asked her, reaching over her to grab some of the crunchies off the chicken. Slapping my hand away as she had always done, I laughed licking my finger.

"I'll be better when you stop digging your dirty hands in my food, Asaad." Being the only child, me and my mother were very close. On most nights, while my father, Frankie, ran the streets it was just the two of us.

"Aight, well then you good. You need anything?"

Turning on her heels, she wiped her hands on the kitchen towel that laid on the counter. "As a matter a fact I do need something, when you and Gabby giving me grandbabies?"

"I'm getting a divorce." The look of disappointment was evident on my mother's face.

"That's a conversation for another day, your father is hawking over us." Looking over my shoulder, I saw my father standing there with his arms folded over his chest.

"Yeah," leaving out of the kitchen I followed him to the den. Most of our conversations were held down here, the less my mother knew the better it was for her. "So what's this about?"

"What's the girl's name? I heard she was engaged to the muthafucka Hass."

"Yeah pops, she was, but she wasn't feeling him." Stopping

at the bar, I poured myself a shot of Henny. Looking over, Chinx was in the reclining chair rolling up a new blunt.

"I don't give a fuck if she was feeling him or not, the fact that she was fucking the enemy should tell you something." Sitting down on the sofa, he continued, "You think the bitch got your back? Cuz you already got enough shit going on with Gabby." Downing the shot, my phone vibrated. Looking down at it, I saw a message from Lou.

Lou: missing you

Smiling, I put the phone on the bar. Turning on the barstool, my father was glaring at me.

"That's the bitch texting you?"

"C'mon pops, why she gotta be all that?" I asked, twisting up my lip at him, shaking my head.

"Cuz she playing both sides, do she know you the one who killed her nigga?"

"Oh her ass knows that shit, she was there!" Chinx doubled over laughing, looking at him as if he was a fucking fool.

"Shut the fuck up Chinx, have you told pops that your ass trying to smash Misha's thick ass?" The look on my father's face was priceless. Jumping up, he popped Chinx in the head.

"I told y'all asses she's off fucking limits. She is not to be touched at all!" The seriousness in my father's voice caused us to both stop laughing.

"Shit, you act like I got her pregnant Unc, I'm just trying to get in where I fit in." Before Chinx could get the rest of the words out his mouth, my father had him by the collar of his shirt. "Damn my bad, so I guess her cousin is off limits too, huh?"

My father let go of Chinx, getting up from kneeling, he looked between the both of us. "Cousin? Misha ain't got no fucking cousin," my father spewed with a mix of rage on his face.

"Pops, that's who I'm talking to."

"Lashay's ass ain't got no kids, it was only them two, no other siblings, so how the fuck she Misha's cousin?"

"Maybe your bitch had another kid, Frankie!" my mother said coldly, peeking her head into the den, staring at my father. The look of disgust was evident on her face. Turning to walk away, my mother told me I better not be around her. Looking from my father to my mother, Chinx got up to leave out.

"I'ma let y'all talk about this shit." Leaving out of the den, my mother followed behind Chinx.

My father sat on the sofa with his hand rubbing against his chin, his eyebrows furrowed as he let out a long sigh. "Asaad, I need to meet the girl; I need to see her and make sure she ain't Lyla's child."

"She is, but I'll tell her to come over now." Pulling out my phone, I dialed Lou's number, "Hey shorty, I'ma give you an address I need you to come here."

"Is everything okay, Saad?"

"Yeah." Ending the call, I looked over at my father.

"I'll explain everything when she gets here."

"Her name is Lou," I added grabbing the cognac off the bar with two shot glasses.

Waiting on Lou to show up, there was an awkward silence that filled the den. My father wouldn't even look in my direction and I couldn't get passed what my mother had said to him. For as long as I could remember, my parents were high school sweethearts, married straight out of high school. Hearing her say *his bitch* had me wanting to ask a bunch of questions. It was obvious my father had cheated on my mother, but the fact that my mother felt so strong about Lou's mother showed that it was more than just a fuck.

Hearing my mother call my name, I hopped up from the stool and headed upstairs. Lou was standing by the door looking uneasy as my mother stared at her. Rubbing her elbows, Lou tapped her foot impatiently. My mother was leaning up against the wall in the kitchen. Lou was standing by the door, not even fully welcomed into the house.

"Hey shorty, come on in." Lou walked into my open arms, looking back at my mother, she rolled her eyes at Lou. Pushing Lou towards the den, I didn't need my mother unleashing any of her hate for her mother on Lou. Opening the door, my father now had the bright light on as he sat on the barstool at the door. Lou looked back at me before entering the room.

"I'll be fucking damned!" he said, getting up and walking in our direction. Staring at Lou, she screwed up her face.

"What is the problem, Asaad? Cuz he's freaking me out." Her southern accent came out heavy as she side eyed me.

"Your mother's name is Layla?"

"Yes, why, did you know her?" Lou asked, softening her face.

"How old are you?" he asked, still staring at her like he knew her.

"Pops listen, cut to the chase, you're scaring her, damn."

"I'm twenty-seven, how do you know my mother?"

"So, Misha is three years older than you, makes perfect sense."

"Okay, someone gonna tell me what the hell is going on or we gonna keep up this secret?"

"Relax lil' mama. Damn, you are the spitting image of Lyla."

"Apparently, my father and your mother fucked with each other."

"Before she got married?"

"No," looking down at the floor, my father sighed heavily. "I need to see Misha and then I can have this conversation with y'all together."

"No, because my father said that shit recently and didn't tell us shit, so I want to know what the fuck is going on!" Lou shouted at the top of her lungs.

"Yeah, tell her how you had a long affair with that little

bitch Lyla," my mother said from behind us with tears in her eyes. "Six years, Frankie, six fucking years."

Lou turned to look at my mother, shaking her head, she let go of my hand before running up the stairs and out of the house. Turning around to run after her, my father told me to bring Misha and Lou over tomorrow to talk.

28

LOU

Running out of the house, my heart was racing. Unable to stop my hands from shaking to dial Misha's number, I dropped my phone on the ground. Reaching down to pick it up, tears spilled out of my eyes. Trying to catch my breath, Asaad grabbed me from behind. Pushing him off of me, he held me tighter.

"Lou calm down, talk to me."

"No, you set me up. Like how, Asaad?" Turning around, I balled up my fist, hitting him in his chest. Feeling like my chest was getting tight, I gripped it, bending over. "Asaad, why didn't you tell me?"

"Lou, I just found out babe.... I just found out."

"Lies! That's why you preyed on me? Like was this a part of your plan?" *How could my mother mention this name to me in a dream and yet I brushed it off like it was nothing?* This shit was more wicked than I could have ever imagined. Frankie, the name on the paper, he and my mother had a history. Now, it was all beginning to make sense.

Backing up from him, I turned to run away. Dialing Misha's number, she answered on the first ring.

"Misha, I'm coming to you! I have to talk to you!"

"I need to talk to you too." It sounded like Misha was crying, but I was so wrapped up in my own emotions that I paid hers no mind. Ordering an Uber, Asaad was walking up the block.

"Stay the fuck away from me Asaad! I want nothing to do with you or your family!"

"Lou, I had nothing to do with the past! I love you!"

"Fuck you! Fuck you and your twisted family!" Spotting the Uber pull up, I opened the door before Asaad could stop me from leaving. Hearing him tell me he loved me struck something inside of me. Shaking my head, I got in the Uber. As it pulled off, I looked out the back window, looking at him.

The ride to Misha's apartment was taking forever, texting my father, I cursed him out terribly before placing him on the block call list. If I had been allowed to visit New York as often as I wanted, then I probably would know the truth behind my mother and father. The fact that Misha was not my cousin but my sister pissed me off. *What type of parent raises one child and not the other?* I thought, just as the car pulled up to Misha's building. I was raised in a loving household with both parents until my mother was killed on the streets. So why the fuck was Misha living in New York with my aunt?

Running up the stairs to the apartment, I began banging on the door, my aunt opened the door just before I could bang again. "What is the damn emergency, Lucy?"

"I need some answers, like right fucking now!"

My aunt snapped her neck in my direction, "First of all, don't come up here cursing in my presence Lucy, and second of all your damn father owes you them answers since my sister is no longer here."

"I don't care who gets me the answers." Pacing the floor, I looked over at Misha whose eyes were puffy and red from crying. My aunt had her phone on speaker as it rung until the caller answered.

"Your ass needs to be in New York and quick!" she spat into the line before hanging up.

Throwing my hands up in the air, I gave her the *what they fuck* look. Another knock on the door caused my aunt to run and open it. Seeing my father stand there looking defeated, I rolled my eyes so hard I felt them in the top of my head.

"Lucy, girl I swear I'm on the verge of knocking ya head off your shoulders." Moving out of his way, I folded my arms over my chest.

"What is going on? So, Misha is my sister, are you her father?"

Shaking his head no, he looked up at Misha who looked out the window. "No I'm not her father, but she is Lyla's daughter."

"So, explain to us how the hell we were separated and raised as cousins instead?"

"Your mother," before he could finish the statement, my aunt told him don't speak ill of her sister who isn't here to defend herself. "Like I was saying, your mother and me were together since we were teens, living in New York." Misha looked over at us. "She ended up pregnant with Misha, and well I told her I wasn't going to continue the marriage if she had the baby, so she gave her to Lashay."

"Back the fuck up and give us the details. If she's not your daughter, then who's her father and how the fuck you give her that ultimatum?" Vexed, I was now yelling at the top of my lungs. Misha was still quiet, but I was tired of beating around the bush for answers.

"She said she was attacked and she ended up pregnant. I couldn't deal with her having a baby by someone who attacked her."

"So, why not let her go?" Misha asked from the other side of the room.

"I loved her too much to let her go," he said hanging his head low.

"Bullshit Oliver, you knew leaving Lyla meant losing out on all that fucking fast money she was bringing in."

"Really Lashay, you gotta go there?"

"Yes, I'm going there cuz you not about to make my sister look like she was this worthless woman and she wasn't." Turning to look at me and Misha, my aunt told us her version. "Listen, y'all's mother was running the streets, heavy into the fast life." Catching her breath, she continued, "she ran with Frankie and his boys growing up. Selling weed and what not and well, when she ended up pregnant with Misha, she was with this low life over here who was back then a cop and he told her she had to get rid of Misha."

Looking over at my father, I shook my head in disgust, he was starting to make me hate the man who I looked up to as my hero. I swore he took on this major role of being a single father and never letting me slip in life only to find out he had a bunch of skeletons in his closet. Unable to stomach the sight of him, I left out the room and returned with my suitcase.

"I'm not even going to do this with you right now, stay out of my life. Misha, I'm only a phone call away, but this sick and twisted family I can't deal with right now." Turning around, I pulled the suitcases I had, stacking one on another, hoping I wouldn't drop my belongings. My father reached out to grab my shoulder, but I shook him off of me. "I'm very serious, stay away." Leaving out of the apartment, I spotted Asaad's car parked in the parking lot. Wanting to avoid him, I decided to go out the back of the building. Getting in an Uber, I headed to the nearest, cheapest hotel. Holding in all of my emotions, I looked at the pictures in my phone of me and my mother growing up.

Notification after notification from Asaad caused me to place my phone on airplane mode. With all the lies that came out today, I didn't even care who Misha's father was, I was mad we shared a mother and she never had the experiences I had. Getting out the Uber and situated in a cheap room, I dropped my suitcases by the door. Closing it, I fell up against it letting out my tears. In this moment, I wanted my mother to tell me everything was a lie and Misha was really my aunt's child. After crying for what seemed like an hour, I pulled myself off the floor, heading in the bathroom. I showered and got in the bed. Thinking about the day my mother was killed, I could only see the black car pull up and the window roll down, then two shots were let off in her direction. Wiping my nose, I tossed and turned until I finally fell asleep.

29

MISHA

Unable to accept all the news that was brought to light, I was pissed off and hurt. The woman I loved like an aunt was my mother, and I still didn't know who my father was. Now understanding why Oliver hated me made sense. My real aunt Lashay told me that she was unable to have children and when Lyla asked her to raise me, she jumped at the idea. I didn't have a hard life, but I damn sure didn't have the life Lucy had. She was spoiled to the point where I would always be jealous when she would call and tell me about all the shit she was doing. Don't get me wrong, I wanted for nothing, I had the latest gear and I went to the best schools, but I didn't get the lavish trips like her. I guess that was my mother's way of showing her love for me.

I should have known something was up when it was my sweet sixteen and Oliver sent a large amount of money to my aunt for me. The day my mother was killed, I remember Lashay getting the call and breaking down. You would have thought someone ripped her heart out of her body. She just kept saying it was that selfish bastard who got her mixed-up in the shit but I couldn't understand how. The minute Oliver left out of the apartment, I looked over at her and asked her, "So, do you know who my father is?"

Watching my aunt sit down on the sofa, she told me to come join her. Taking my hands in hers, she told me she loved me and would never lie to me from this day forward. I knew she loved me without a doubt, she raised me as if I was her own child. "Don't ever once think that Lyla didn't love you because girl, she loved everything about you." Smiling, she shook her head, holding back the tears. "I remember the day she came in and told me she was pregnant; she was happy as hell and the glow was evident on her face." Sighing, she continued, "But she wasn't pregnant by her abusive ass husband, she was pregnant by her long time crush, Frankie."

Widening my eyes in shock, I asked, "What? So, Asaad is my brother?"

"Listen, so she wanted to tell Frankie she was pregnant by him, but the day she went to tell him was the day his wife Sharee found out about them." Letting go of my hands, she looked at me. "Yeah, so she just said fuck it, she wasn't going to tell him, even though I told her it wasn't a good idea. Any who, she kept you a secret until she began showing and Oliver started questioning shit."

"So, that's when she made up the story, huh?"

"Yeah, so she told him she was attacked by some dude and she was too scared to tell him who because she knew he would go searching." Laying my head back on the sofa, I massaged my temples.

"After weeks, Oliver told her that she had to get rid of you, but she wasn't having it. She told him she was going to have you and he better accept it. Anyway, she asked me if I wanted to raise you as my own, being I couldn't and I jumped at the idea." Unable to be upset with my aunt, I was grateful for her taking me in, but now having more answers about Frankie, I reached out to Lou to see if she would take a trip with me. After a few minutes of the message not being sent, I tried calling her only to be sent straight to voicemail.

"She acts like she's the only one hurt," I mumbled to no one in particular. Drained, I ended up going in my room and calling Asaad. The minute he answered, I told him I needed to go see Frankie. He told me to be ready in thirty minutes.

Getting dressed, I waited outside on the stoop smoking a blunt. Taking a pull from it, Asaad walked up on me with Chinx in tow.

"What are you doing here?" Rolling my eyes at him, Asaad took the blunt from my hand, smoking it.

"Listen shorty, I'm trying to go there with you, but Frankie ain't having that shit, so I gotta fall back."

"You blood to Frankie or nah?"

"Nah, but he like my family, so I gotta respect it." Getting up off the stoop, I wiped the dirt off my ass before walking in the direction of the car. Tapping on the hood of the car, Asaad unlocked the door. Hopping in, I waited for him and Chinx to finish the blunt. Laying my head back, I needed my nerves calmed. This wouldn't be my first time around Frankie, so I didn't understand why I was so anxious. I guess the thought of finding out if he is my father or not was scaring me. The minute they got in the car, Asaad asked me if I was good. Nodding my head, he asked where Lou was. I shrugged my shoulders.

"I don't know and honestly she's acting like she the only one who found out some shit today."

"I mean, I can get her frustration, but yeah she is acting up if she shutting you out. I'm just trying to go get my girl back cuz I love your sis." Smiling at him, I could tell he really did love my sister in just that short amount of time, but with him still being married I wasn't about to let her follow in our mother's footsteps.

The drive to the house was quiet outside of the radio playing music. I caught Chinx looking at me through the mirror a few times. Every time I rolled my eyes at him. Pulling into the driveway, Frankie was outside on the porch.

"I hope my mother ain't kick his ass out." All of us busted out laughing when we saw a suitcase beside him on the porch.

"Yo Pops, what's going on?"

"Man, Sharee in there tripping. She know I can't go be with Lyla, yet she done told me to go be with her."

Asaad thought it was funny cuz he began laughing at him, dragging his suitcase to the house, he unlocked the door. Being stopped by the chair, he shouted through the door to his mother.

"Asaad, I hope you don't have that piece of a shit father with you!"

"Ma c'mon, you know he loves you. How long has it been since Lyla passed away?"

"Asaad, I don't give a damn cuz had he not of shot her that day then guess what, he would still be with her!" Stepping back from the porch, I looked at Frankie who looked down at the ground.

"You killed my mother?"

"Misha, it's not as simple as she's saying it. Listen, I loved your mother with every breath in me, but the minute I found out she was about to snitch on me, I had no choice Misha."

"You killed my mother in front of her child at a park. What type of fucking monster are you?" I shouted as the tears ran down my face. Lunging forward in his direction, Chinx caught me. Grabbing me into a bear hug, he held onto me as I unleashed blow after blow. "You sit here talking about you loved her and you killed her! She had two children and to think you're my fucking father!"

"What?" Asaad shouted, turning around just as his mother flew right by him and smacked the shit out of Frankie. Unable to protect himself, he fell on the ground as Sharee hit him over and over.

"You got that bitch pregnant! This whole time you had me helping you raise your fucking illegitimate child!" This shit was too much for me to handle right now. Turning around, I took off down the block. Stopping at the corner, I looked back at Asaad and his mother shout at Frankie who looked helpless. Sitting down on the curb, I cried until Chinx sat beside me and held me.

"Shorty, this shit is messy as fuck. Let me get you outta here and to your peoples." Following behind him in a daze, I rode to my house. Turning to leave, I never looked back.

Racing back to the house, I buried my face into my hands, leaning up against the door. Lifting my head up, I banged it against the back of the door until I could bring myself back to reality. Dragging my feet against my tiled floors, I looked in my boys' room. Noticing they weren't there, I walked across to my room. A pale yellow envelope laid on my dresser, catching my attention. Looking over my shoulder, I had to think who else would have come by here besides my mom.

"Damn sure wasn't Don coming by."

Picking it up, I strolled over to my bed, anxiously ripping it open from the top. A folded letter was inside. Dropping the envelope on the floor, I pulled back the old white paper. My eyes widened when I read the first line.

Hey Misha. It's your mother, Lyla.

Sitting still for a minute, I had to process what I just read. Rereading over the letter aloud, I grew more pissed with Oliver for his role in my mother's death. Not only was he abusive on the regular but he had told her she had to set up Frankie or he was going to turn into her worse enemy.

Falling back onto my bed, I sunk into my plush comforter, holding the letter up. Feeling my stomach turn, a rush of vomit tried to escape my lips. I placed my hand over my mouth, trying to hold it down. Stepping on something on the floor, I ran into the bathroom releasing everything on the floor. Hunched over,

I breathed in and out, clearing my throat. The smell of the vomit mixed with the food I had earlier assaulted my nostrils. Standing straight, I grabbed a towel from the bar on the wall. Picking up the vomit and hoping to not throw up again from the sight and smell of it, I jumped in the shower.

Staggering in the room feeling light headed, I saw a black object on the floor under the envelope. Bending down, I picked up a small, black usb drive. Looking around the room for my old Dell laptop, I plugged it in. Seeing my mother's face plastered on the screen with purple and black bruises, I listened as she whispered into the computer. She kept looking over her shoulder; the fear was evident on her face as she bit down on her lip.

Hearing Oliver yell in the background, she continued to whisper. Trying to decipher what room she was in; I noticed the tiled walls.

"He's so crazy. I swear," she mumbled, *coming closer to the screen. "I'm sure I'm not going to make it much longer because I can't stand him. I am in love with Frankie."*

Hearing the door open, the screen went black. I could hear her screaming no, and I couldn't contain my anger. Burying my face into the comforter, I cried. There was no way I could show Lou this; it would kill her. Rolling over on my back, I stared into the pattern of chippings on the ceiling, allowing the tears to trickle down my face until I became numb.

30

ASAAD

After shouting all the shit to my father, I shook my head before walking away. Trying to hold back the tears, I felt as a man I shouldn't be crying, but the shit was fucked up. The perfect life I had growing up spiraled out of control in a flash. Feeling my phone vibrate in my pocket, I saw the notification on my Facebook app light up. It was a message from Gabby. Sitting in my car, I unlocked my phone and saw a few messages from her.

Gabby: can you unblock me?

Gabby: Asaad I need to talk to you.

Gabby: Asaad please I need to talk to you.

Gabby: okay I get it you want this divorce but I want to raise our baby with two parents, (inserts pregnancy test picture)

Sucking my teeth, I threw my phone at the dashboard. Hitting my window leaving a small crack. I didn't want no children with Gabby now, and the fact that she picked the worse fucking time to get pregnant was mind blowing. All these years, I wanted her to sit her ass down and get pregnant, yet she swore by them birth control pills. Now, I'm ready for a divorce; in love with Lou, and she sends me this shit. Starting up the car, I drove until I couldn't drive anymore that night. Parking by Central Park, I took out my phone scrolling to Lou's name, hoping she didn't have me blocked. Her phone went straight to voicemail. Hitting the steering wheel, I bit my lip making it bleed. "Fuck!" Reaching over, I found some tissue cleaning my lip. Feeling my phone vibrate, it was my mother calling. Ignoring her call, she called again.

"Yes!"

"Your father had a heart attack Asaad, please come home!" she cried into the line while her voice was shaking. Starting up the car, I called Misha, I knew she probably wouldn't give a fuck, but I didn't want to not tell her what was going on.

"Yeah," she answered in a groggily tone, clearing her throat.

"Misha my father, I mean our father had a heart attack."

"You're telling me why? I don't know him as my father. I'm sorry that happened, but yeah I'm not inserting myself. He killed my mother." Hanging up in my ear before I could respond, I tried calling Lou again. Being sent to voicemail again, I rode the rest of the way in silence. Driving straight to the hospital after asking my mother which hospital he was taken to. Rushing through the hallways, I asked where he was being seen at. Spotting my mother in the waiting area, her eyes were puffy from crying. Gabby walked out of the bathroom just as I got closer to my mother. Mumbling under my breath, I could have killed my mother.

"What are you doing here?"

"He's my father-in law Asaad; just because you on some shit don't mean your parents are." Wanting to grab her up and toss her out of the hospital, I pulled my mother in my embrace. Allowing her to cry into my chest, I heard Chinx make his entrance.

"You good?" Patting me on my back, I told him I was good. Taking my mother to one of the seats, we sat and waited for an update. Gabby kept looking in my direction from across me. Getting up, she took the empty seat on my left. Holding onto my arm, I nudged her off of me.

"Just because you're here doesn't mean you can touch me, Gabby."

"Asaad, that is your wife, don't lose her over no skank."

"Whatever ma, she's a damn gold digger and the woman you met earlier is everything but that." Gabby gasped, clapping her hand over her mouth as her eyes widened.

"You took her to meet your mother?"

"Gabby, don't do this shit right now; my father just had a heart attack for Christ sake!" Walking off and leaving her there, she soon followed behind me.

"Asaad, I'm pregnant, so you're still leaving?"

"I don't give a damn; I'ma be there for my child but I refuse to stay with you because you're having my fucking child!" Storming off, she was getting under my skin. Texting Chinx to let me know when the doctor came out to update them, I waited in my car.

Thirty minutes later and Chinx was calling me, jumping out of my car I ran through the halls to where my mother and the rest of them were waiting. Seeing the small smile on my mother's face, I knew my father had made it through. Telling them I didn't want to see him; I'd call instead, I left out of the hospital.

31
———

LOU

Removing myself from the world, I literally shut everyone out. Disconnecting my phone, I stayed at the Opera Hotel on 149th street and 3rd avenue for a week before I found a room to rent out in Brooklyn. After crying for a few months for my mother to come and save me from the pain, I had to drag myself out of bed. My funds were getting low and I could no longer afford to stay in the hotel.

Finding a job as a daycare teacher, I had started to gain back some independence. Feeling sick day in and day out, I finally got the courage to get up and make a doctor's appointment. Finding out I was pregnant was the worst news I could have gotten. I swore I had a stomach virus when I couldn't keep anything down, but then I couldn't remember the last time I had my period. Cursing out myself in the bathroom, I told myself I was not aborting the baby.

Unlocking my door to my room, I kicked off my shoes and tossed my purse on the bed. Remembering it was Misha's birthday, I signed into the WIFI account and opened up my Instagram. Searching through the photos on my phone I made a six picture collage of us growing up and wished her a happy birthday. Tagging her in the picture, so she would get the message, I closed out of the app. Tossing my phone on the bed, I removed the orange maxi dress I had on. Looking at my body in the mirror, I saw the little pouch that began to form. The sonogram I was given told me I was thirteen weeks pregnant. Overwhelmed with emotion, I touched my stomach, wanting to feel any type of movement to let me know I was making the right choice. I figured, what did I have to lose? I had no one and right about now I wanted to feel loved. Hearing a ding on my phone I grabbed it up.

Misha replied, "Thanks but this is a shitty way to tell me sis, don't you think?"

Rolling my eyes, I flopped down on the bed. Going back and forth between if I should just call her or not, I dialed her number. She answered on the second Instagram video call.

"Oh, look who it is from the dead."

"Misha I'm sorry but I'm going through a lot and—" Before I could dump my sorrow on her, she told me to shut up.

"First of all, did you stop to think about me during this process, Lou? I didn't have my mother nor my father and you had both until my father apparently killed mommy." Screwing up my face, she had lost me.

"What?"

"Yes, if you wouldn't have shut me out, you would have found out that Frankie is my father and he killed our mother because she was about to snitch on him." The feeling of hurt and anger overcame me. Unable to hold back the tears, I dropped my phone on the floor. Misha continued talking until she heard me sobbing.

"Lou, where are you? I'm coming over." No longer wanting to hide where I was, I ran off my address to her.

Getting up to unlock the door, I crawled back into bed. Burying my face into the pillow, Misha walked in about forty-five minutes later.

"Lou I'm so sorry." Climbing into the bed behind me, she held me as I cried until I no longer had any tears. "Lou, you know you leaving me scared the shit out of me?" Turning to face Misha, I saw the tears falling from her eyes. Pulling her in to hug her, I now allowed her to cry.

"I'm sorry Misha, I didn't mean to scare you. I just was hurt and didn't know how to deal with it." Wiping her face, she got up from the bed. Walking to the bathroom to wipe her face she came back holding the sonogram.

"Are we expecting a baby?"

Smiling for the first time in a while, I nodded my head yes. Misha ran over to me, trying to look at my small belly, she rubbed on it. "I'ma be a Titi!" Taking in all of her excitement, I grew quiet.

"It's Asaad's baby. I'm not sure if I want him to know."

Covering her mouth with her hand, she replied, "He doesn't need to know cuz it's been put out there that his wife is carrying his fucking baby." When Misha dropped that bomb on me, I got up off the bed, and rushed to the bathroom. Kneeling over the toilet, I threw up the sandwich I had earlier. Staying in the bathroom, I hopped in the shower trying to pull myself together. Misha banged on the bathroom door, making me cut the shower off.

"Lou, fuck him. You don't need him."

"I can't believe this shit." Pulling open the door, I had the gray towel wrapped around my body. "Yet he told me 'Oh I'm divorcing her Lou, I love you'," I impersonated him the best way I could. "Fuck outta here with that bullshit." Pacing back and forth, Asaad had pissed me off and didn't even know it.

"Don't let him get you upset, you wanna go fuck him up?" Looking over at Misha, I began laughing at her.

"You serious?" I asked Misha, noticing she wasn't laughing.

"Yep, he's my brother, so I know he ain't gonna do shit

anyway." Shrugging her shoulders, she sat on the bed pulling out her phone.

"Don't call him Misha, please. I'm not ready to deal with him." Feeling uneasy in my stomach, I begged her to keep her mouth shut. Agreeing, she asked me how I was overall. Looking around the room she turned her nose up.

"I know your bougie ass ain't alright cuz you ain't never lived in no fucking box." Laughing, I shook my head at her. She was right, I had subjected myself to living like this to avoid Asaad. "I can help you find an apartment since you got a job and it's in the city, so you're good."

"I know, but I want to do this on my own. Before Hassel, I was living lavish with my dad and then I met Asaad." Stopping at the mention of his name, I became sad, "I miss him Misha, I loved his thuggish ass."

"So, call him Lucy."

"He's married and having a baby, Misha."

"And he's in love with your ass and you're having his baby. Shittin' me, you better go get ya nigga."

Thinking about what Misha was saying; yeah it was true, but I wasn't ready to face him and the reality of what was going on. Getting tired, I asked her if she was staying over. When she told me she was, we got dressed and went down the block to go celebrate her birthday at the famous Jamaican restaurant "Footprints". After she had a few drinks I was ready to leave. It was a Friday and I couldn't enjoy the fun of drinking.

"Bitch nobody told you to be bustin' it open with no protection." Cracking up, I told her to shut the hell up. After another drink, I was ready to call it a night. Once we were in my room, I watched her sleep while I sat up thinking about Asaad. *Damn, I want one of his hugs right now*, I thought as I eventually got in the bed beside Misha.

32
____

ASAAD

Sitting in the prenatal appointment with Gabby, she talked about all the what if's, "Assad what if we had a girl? What would we name her?"

She was annoying me. Just thinking about her pushing out my child stressed me out. My mother pushed rekindling a relationship with her, but it was too much damage done. She definitely wasn't talking about working now that she was pregnant, she wanted to be a stay at home mom. I would have agreed if she wasn't so comfortable with me taking care of her. She was literally giving me a headache talking about the future. Putting a hold on the divorce until I got a DNA test on the baby, which sent her into a fit of rage, I wanted to know if the baby was mine. My father didn't agree with the test either, but had he gotten the shit on Misha we would have known about her sooner.

Hearing the doctor call her name, she jumped up pulling on my arm. I wanted to be happy but it was too late for me to feel anything towards Gabby. She'd bleached my clothing, tore up my sneakers and even got my parents involved in her bullshit after posting up videos drunk talking shit about me. Walking behind her, I rubbed on my beard, "Gabby relax, we gonna get to the room, damn." I should have been excited; we were finding out the sex of the baby today, but instead, I only thought about how Lou was. She had literally disappeared; her phone was disconnected and she wasn't keeping in contact with Misha either. Hoping she was good, I missed holding her small ass. She was really the peace I needed in my life, yet I was stuck with a crazy bitch like Gabby.

"Hey parents," the doctor greeted us. Sitting in the chair as usual, I looked on as the doctor gave Gabby her sonogram. Hearing the baby's heartbeat always sent a calm wave over me. Placing the tool on Gabby's stomach, I looked on at the small screen. "It's a boy!" Jumping up excited, I pumped my fist at the ceiling. Shit, I ain't expect to get so excited at the thought of carrying on my legacy. Gabby looked at me smiling with admiration in her eyes, unable to feel the type of love she had towards me, I knew in that moment regardless, I was going to make sure her and my son was always good.

Helping her up from the bed, she got down after cleaning her stomach off. Taking her to lunch and then to my parents' house, I got a call from Chinx to meet him in the hood. Knowing that it was more than likely some shit popping off, I grabbed my nine and left out. Saying a quick prayer, I left out the house. Jumping in the car, I drove to the hood where I spotted Chinx posted up against the fence. Looking over to the right of him I saw one of the young boys who used to sell for us. His lip was bloodied and his eye was black.

Leaving my nine in the car when I saw who we were talking to, I walked up on them. "What's going on?"

"Yo, tell the boss man the shit you told me Lee."

Lee looked down at the ground before looking back up in my direction. Licking his lips, he touched it with his right hand.

"I told Chinx my work got taken by some muthafucka from

out of state, and he told me to let you know he was coming for you." Walking up on Lee, I stooped down to his five foot eight inch frame. Tapping his chest, I asked him to repeat himself. The minute he opened his mouth to repeat himself, I punched him in his chest. Sending him flying back into the black fence he held onto his chest.

"Lee, I'ma need a lil' more information from your ass, so get the fuck back over here." Hearing cars screeching on the block, I fixated my attention on Lee who was he trying to get up off the ground.

"Put your hands up, Asaad!" one of the officers shouted from his car. Turning around, I saw a row of cars. Spotting him in the front, I ran my tongue over my teeth.

"Asaad, don't do nothing stupid, this can be easy or you can go down trying to get away."

"Oliver, this how you want to do shit? You mad cuz ya daughter fell in love with the kid?" Taunting him with the thought of me and Lou, he flared his nose.

"Asaad, just bring your ass on, my daughter ain't fucking with you."

"Says who?"

"The bitch we got to set you up!" Looking at the cars, I tried to see if I recognized anyone.

"I ain't got shit to hide my nigga, you mad cuz ya daughter love me and your wife was in love with my father." Sending him over the edge, Oliver ran up on me knocking me down. Before I could really get a good hit in, we were rushed by the cops. Grabbing me up, they placed me in handcuffs, "Yo, Chinx go call my lawyer and my pops." People had their cameras out recording everything that was going on. Oliver punched me; blood flew from my mouth.

"You lucky old man, you a lucky son of a bitch!" I spat in his direction missing his foot.

Being thrown in the back of the car I cursed out all the officers who had something to do with my arrest. Laying my head back, I flared my nose looking in the rearview mirror at my bloodied mouth.

33

LOU

The banging on my room door scared me out of my sleep. Jumping up, I looked around for a weapon. Hoping it wasn't one of the other tenants starting no shit, I crept to the door. Hearing Misha's voice, I pulled back the door. Looking at her and Chinx standing there, I widened my eyes at her. I had let Misha come back in my life three months ago and she had followed my wishes of not letting Asaad or Chinx know where I laid my head. Closing my robe tighter over my small baby bump, I moved to the side so they could come in.

Chinx looked me over with worry on his face. Closing the door, Misha told me to sit down. Doing as she told me, I sat there looking at the both of them up and down. Waiting on one of them to open their mouths first, I snapped my fingers in their direction.

"Y'all wanna tell me why y'all woke me up out of my sleep?"

"Asaad got arrested and your dad is the reason he's there."

Looking perplexed, I asked them to clarify what they were telling me. "Lucy, your father has been following your baby father for a minute," when Misha said that, I jumped up off the bed.

"What?" forgetting all the hatred I tried to have against Asaad, I went in my bathroom and got dressed. Coming out with a T-shirt and leggings on, I followed them out to the car. Without asking any more questions, I cut on my phone and dialed my father's number. After the third ring, he answered the phone.

"Oh let me guess, you heard about that fucking boy, huh?"

"So you really had him arrested? Do you know how much you are making me hate the muthafucka you are?"

"Lucy, you really running behind this thug when he don't give a fuck about nobody but the streets like his father!"

"You're just mad because apparently mom loved him more than she ever loved you!"

"If that's the case, then why the fuck was she about to snitch on him? Huh?" The question caught me off guard, because Misha did mention that she was about to snitch on him. "Fuck all that, I'm having his baby, so whether you like it or not, we share something!" Ending the call before he could piss me off further, I kicked the back of the seat where Misha was sitting. She turned to me and asked if I was good. Breaking down into tears, I couldn't be strong any longer.

The man I was in love with was at war with my first love; my father. My mother had been killed by his father all because she had to choose between my father and him. I was breaking the cycle; I wasn't choosing my father. I was choosing the man I loved and carried his child in me for the past five months. Pulling up at the courthouse, I waited until I heard Asaad's name being called. Jumping up, I looked at his mother and his father who stared at me. Wiping my face, I walked into the courtroom with Misha and Chinx by my side. Seeing the back of Asaad standing next to his lawyer, I held my head down when I felt my father's eyes burning a hole in me.

"Assad do you have any request?"

"Listen, your honor, yes I have done some foul shit back in the days, but I run a lucrative real estate building."

"I understand that, but from my documents, it shows you are also a menace to society."

"How when I haven't killed a soul?"

"You killed Hassel, fuck you taking about!" My father shouted in Assad's direction.

"No, he didn't daddy, I keep telling you that!" Misha covered my mouth as everyone turned in my direction. Unable to keep my comments to myself, I tried breaking free of Misha and Chinx's grasp. "He didn't kill that low down dirty muthafucka!"

"Order in the court. Ma'am, I'm going to have to ask you to keep it together before I hold you in contempt."

Looking over at Asaad, our eyes met. He shook his head at me before looking down at my growing belly. Forcing a smile, he lifted his finger over his mouth, motioning for me to hush. Closing my eyes, I took a seat, laying my head on the headrest in front of me. I heard the charges they ran off. Second degree murder and possession of drugs. Sobbing, Misha rubbed the small of my back. Not wanting to continue and listen to the charges, I jumped up, "I hate you! I swear I hate you!"

"Guard, please hold this young lady in contempt!" Slamming down on the gravel, the officer came to take me out of the courtroom. I heard my father shouting for the judge to let me go, but he wasn't having it. Looking at Asaad, he blew a kiss in my direction before I was led out of the courtroom.

Being placed in a cell, I sat on the bench laying my head against the wall. Closing my eyes, I thought about how my whole life was really a lie because my father wanted shit the way he wanted it. After sitting in the cell for what seemed like hours, I saw Frankie walking towards the cell with Sharee. Rolling my eyes, I turned my back to them.

"Lucy, I'm sorry for how these last months have been, but my son asked for me to get you out, so here I am."

Shaking my head no, I ignored him as Sharee talked to me through the bars. My father walked up with one of the cops. They opened the cell and told me to come out. I only got up to go and slap my father across his face. "I told you I couldn't stand you and if I am free because of any of you foul mutha-fuckas, I'd rather stay locked up!" Turning to go back to the cell, Sharee blurted out that Asaad was free on bail. Hearing that made my ears perk up and my heart melt.

"Where is he?"

"He's outside waiting on you." Walking out of the cell, I left out of the jailhouse. The minute I laid eyes on Asaad, I walked fast over in his direction. Turning around, he was smiling. Taking me into his embrace, I cried on his chest. "Asaad, why is this shit happening?"

"I can tell you one reason baby, the hate be so real ma, but trust, I got you and my baby." Rubbing his big hands over my small belly, I felt a small wave of kicks for the first time. Getting down on his knees, he lifted the shirt I had on, panting kisses all over my belly. "Damn Lou, that's our baby in there." Looking up at me, I nodded at him.

"Yes Saad, that's our baby." Gabby must have not agreed with the scene, because she started shouting a bunch of bull-shit. Walking behind my father, she told Asaad he could go suck a dick. Asaad shrugged at her and looked back in my direction. Getting up off of his knees, I looked over his tired appearance. Smirking, I playfully hit his arm. "You looking real old baby. You let that bitch stress you out that much that you getting gray hair."

He laughed, kissing the crook of my neck, "Hell yeah, but anyway I'm trying to sleep up inside of that pussy." For the first time in my whole pregnancy, I felt my coochie jump in excitement. Misha told me to go make-up for lost time while she and Chinx disappeared into his car.

Getting in the back of the car with Asaad, I laid my head on his chest. His father drove the car and his mother sat on the passenger seat. For the first time in a long time, I was calm. On the ride to where Asaad now lived, I stayed quiet, hearing his heartbeat as he held onto my stomach. Stopping at his house, I got out the car following behind him. His mother called out to me, turning around to look at her, she told me she had much respect for me for putting up with this and being strong.

Smiling briefly at her, I still didn't like his mother. She only felt this way because she found Gabby to be a snake. Once we were in the house, I stripped down to my underwear, leaving my clothes in all different parts of the house.

"Your ass still ain't learn to clean up behind yourself, huh?" Asaad shouted to my back as I climbed into his king-sized bed. Pulling the Ugg comforter over me, I got comfortable. Asaad slid in behind me tugging at my boy shorts I wore.

Wiggling until I was completely out of the underwear, Asaad lifted my leg and buried his face in my pussy. Gripping his shoulder and hair, I yelled out in pleasure. "Oh my god Asaad! I'm going to cum!" Coming up for air, he slipped his hard dick inside of me. Being as gentle as he could, he grinded inside of me, hitting my g-spot. I opened my mouth yelling out.

"Fuck Lou, this pussy was made for me!" Trying to match his rhythm without causing any discomfort to the baby, I felt my pussy convulsing. Tightening my pussy around his dick, he threw his head back. Feeling his dick jerk inside of me, I creamed all over him. Asaad leaned down, kissing my forehead and then my lips. "Shit baby, I swear I love the shit out of you." Smiling a goofy smile, he pulled out of me before leaving out the room. After he cleaned himself and me, he pulled me into his embrace. With the AC on blast, I snuggled closer to him.

Running my fingers through his beard, I closed my eyes. "Damn, you are really my peace, Lou. All the shit I been through, coming to lay up under you is the most peaceful thing I've felt in a long time." Running my hand up and down his chest, I fell asleep to the rhythm of his heartbeat

34

OLIVER

After leaving the court, I wanted to snatch Lucy's ass up and fuck her up but seeing my baby girl pregnant made me want to grab her and hug her. I had fucked up so much over the years; first I lost my wife to gun violence because I gave her the ultimatum of her snitching or staying with me. The minute she told me she was going to risk it all to be with Frankie, I sent the hit out. Letting the dudes in his camp know that she was going to snitch on him, I just planned for him to turn his back on her. I didn't expect that in a million years that he was going to kill her in broad daylight. Now seeing my daughter fall madly in love with his son, I was not about to lose her to them.

The minute Gabby called me and told me she could help me and also get my daughter back on my good side, I was all ears. I already had my inside man, but when Gabby gave me the operation in full, I was all game. Yeah, I was greedy and yeah, I was all about taking down this whole family, so I jumped at the idea. I never thought I'd see my daughter carrying his baby and professing her love for him in the court-room and risking her freedom. The shit struck a nerve that I wasn't ready to face. Pleading with the judge for leniency for Lucy, he let her go. Instead of coming back to me, her ass still chose that thug.

I met Lyla when I was in the streets, but the minute my mother found out, she warned if I didn't get my shit straight, I was going to be on the streets. Enrolling in the police academy, I begged Lyla to leave the streets behind too, but she was so deep in that it wasn't that simple. I figured I'd marry her and she would give up being Frankie's side bitch and devote herself to me, but I was wrong. The moment she ended up pregnant with Misha, I was devastated. My boys and parents told me I was stupid and clowned me, but I was just in love. Shit, I even think I was content with being in control of Lyla. Telling her to get an abortion was out of the question, so giving the baby to her older sister who couldn't have kids was the best thing to do.

Lyla saw Misha often; I would allow her to take Lou with her sometimes. The last time I told her she couldn't be in New York anymore was the weekend before she was murdered. Lyla ignored my calls that weekend and my baby called me saying she wanted mommy to take her out to eat but she left with a guy. Feeling the blood drain from my face, I jumped up and got on the next flight to New York. Arriving in the night, I used the resources I learned on the job. Tracking her phone, I waited at the apartment building for her to come out. Knowing my wife, she wasn't about to sleep over with him because she brought Lou with her.

Sitting in the black Nissan Altima rental I had, I watched my wife exit the building. Frankie was right behind her, holding onto the back loop of her jeans. Turning her around, she spun in his arms, her long wavy hair blew in the wind, causing her to chuckle. My jaw clenched with each movement of his hand. He bent down and they shared a deep kiss, shit was far from the small pecks she would place all over my face.

"Stupid bitch," I mumbled until he let her go. Hoping he

didn't drive her, a taxi pulled up and they held hands for a few minutes. Leaving him, she turned and blew him a kiss. It was nighttime and I was across the streets but I knew my wife was blushing the minute he blew her a kiss back and she turned to the side lowering her head smiling.

Driving off, I followed the taxi a few blocks until we came to a stop sign, jumping out quickly with my gun. I ran up to the driver's window pointing my gun at him, "Stop the fucking car and get out!" Hearing Lyla scream in shock, she looked at me with tears running down her face.

"Lyla, I'm going to fucking kill you!"

Opening the back door, I pulled her out of the car by her shirt, "You still fucking this nigga?" Now on the floor screaming out in fear, I brought the pistol down crashing her on her shoulder.

"Oliver please, I'm sorry, I'm sorry!" Lyla sobbed as the driver shouted, he was calling the cops before driving off.

Bending down to her level, I slapped her face, splitting her lip. Lyla shielded her face as each blow hit her one after the other. No longer hearing her cry, I backed up breathing heavily. Scared I killed her, I grabbed at her. The amount of blood on her face shocked me. I had blacked out and fucked up my wife. Thinking about my baby girl, I picked up Lyla and placed her in the backseat. Driving until I saw a 24-hour pharmacy, I grabbed up all of the items to clean her off.

Running back to the car, Lyla was moving in slow motion. Looking down at her hands trembling, I got in the car and held her until she stopped crying. I made it my business to tell her to let her sister know she was attacked and Lou needed to stay there for a few days when she called her. Lashay agreed, next she told Frankie she was attacked as well. Shifting her anger to him, she blamed him for not driving her home because he had to go pick up Sharee from her mother's house.

I heard him on the phone begging to see her, but Lyla

ended the call and blocked his number. A few days later, I wanted the attack to seem believable, so I put out word that she was snitching on him to us. We didn't have shit on Frankie and his boys but being that I was a cop and they weren't fucking with each other, it seemed likely to happen. The day Lyla was murdered in the park, I had just dropped off Lou to her and took her luggage to the house. Getting the call might have been one of the worst calls I've ever gotten.

Sitting in the house, sipping some brandy, I thought about Lou being her mother's child without even knowing it. Seeing her stare into Asaad's eyes earlier, it was like looking at her mother and Frankie. Shit scared me; it was wicked. Lifting the glass again, I heard the shower turn off. Watching her come out with a towel wrapped around her body, she smiled in my direction.

"Daddy, I know you're not tripping off that shit!" Sashaying in my direction, she dropped to her knees before unzipping my pants. Laying my head back, I closed my eyes. She opened her mouth taking my semi-erect dick in her mouth.

"Shit Gabby, deep throat that shit!" Grabbing the weave she had on her head, I guided her up and down my dick. Bringing it to a full hard-on she removed my dick from her mouth, licking and sucking my balls. I let out a moan.

"Damn girl," feeling myself about to explode, I told her to back up. Gabby was a nasty bitch, she kept sucking and licking my dick until I exploded in her mouth. Swallowing all of my seeds, she got up from the floor. Watching her belly protrude from the towel, I instantly got pissed. She still didn't know who the father of the baby was, I allowed her to put the baby on Asaad for as long as I could until he got locked up. But I knew the baby she was carrying was mine because she had yet to get pregnant by Asaad in all the years of them being married.

"When you going to look into the fucking DNA test Gabriella?" I asked her, getting up from the chair, pulling up my pants. I looked at her clean her mouth out.

"Oliver, must we go over this every time I see you? It's like damn, can't we enjoy each other's company?"

"No!" Brushing passed her, I cut on the shower. I met Gabby early last year when I was out at a bar in North Carolina with Hassel. She kept eyeing me from the VIP section Asaad had with his people. Knowing who he was because he made it his business to come down here and show off every chance he got, I lifted my glass in her direction. She winked, nodding towards the bathroom. I got up and headed that way after a few minutes. Meeting her by the bathroom, Gabby wasted no time pushing me into the one stall bathroom. Sucking me dry, she swallowed my seeds. Bracing, I gathered myself. Asking for my number, I ran it off to her before leaving out the bathroom. She was cool in the beginning, but then she started throwing up how her husband was mistreating her for some bitch. I didn't realize the chick was my child until the day at the hospital.

Wanting to warn my daughter, she had shut me out. Hearing Gabby snap her fingers in my face, she asked me what I was buying for dinner. Looking around the bedroom, I was disgusted with her, "Gabby why don't you go into the kitchen and cook!"

"Hello, I'm pregnant," she said, pointing to her protruding belly. I sucked my teeth and got up brushing past her.

"You was pregnant when your ass was just on your knees sucking my fucking dick too!" Grabbing up my shirt and shoes, I got dressed before looking for my blazer.

"So, you're leaving, cuz you in your feelings?"

"No, I'm leaving cuz your ass is pathetic; you don't fucking cook or clean. No wonder your husband wants nothing to do with you."

The look of embarrassment was evident on her face. She looked around the house she used to share with Asaad.

"I wasn't pathetic when I was sucking your dick!" she shouted pointing her finger in my face.

"Gabriella, get your hand out of my face before I break it. I don't think you want to try me today." Moving around her, she jumped her ass back in my face, waving her finger. I gripped her wrist. "Gabby, I'm going to hurt you, stop fucking playing." Twisting her wrist, she winced in pain. Before I could black out on her, I thought about the baby she was carrying. Turning around, I left out of the house. Hearing her shout behind me, I kept telling myself to walk away before I end up killing her just because she disrespected me.

Walking down the driveway, I spotted a car creeping up the block. Before I could react, shots fired in my direction. Hitting the pavement hard, I rolled over trying to find a car to duck down under. Gabby must have heard the shooting because she opened the front door calling out to me. The car sped off just as she stepped out of the house. "Gabby are you crazy? Someone is shooting and your pregnant ass comes outside!"

Yelling at her, she stopped mid-stride before screaming, "Oh my god Oliver! Oh my god!" Looking down at her trembling hands, I felt the pain rip through my chest. Feeling my body, the burning sensation caused me to breathe heavily. Looking at my hand, it was covered in blood. Laying my head back against the pavement, I closed my eyes thinking about my daughter and my grandchild she was carrying.

"Shit. I was a fucked up person, but did I deserve this?" Before I could answer my own question, I lost consciousness.

35

LOU

Rolling over in bed to my phone ringing nonstop, I sucked my teeth before looking over to my right and realizing Asaad was gone. Looking down at the phone, it was an unknown caller calling me. Screwing up my face, I answered the phone in a groggy tone.

"Hello."

"Lucy, you have to get to the hospital, your father was shot multiple times and it's not looking good." Sitting up in bed, I tried to decipher the female's voice on the other end. I didn't know if it was pregnancy brain or being woken up out of my sleep, but I couldn't remember where I heard it.

"He was rushed to Lenox Hill, so please get there." The caller hung up and I became pissed all over again.

Sitting up in bed, I pulled back the blankets with force before hopping out of bed. "Where the fuck is Asaad? I swear if he had anything to do with this bullshit, I'm going to fuck him up!" Looking around the room, I found a pair of his basketball shorts. Throwing them on, I tied the string as tight as I could. Thank god I had this belly because he was huge compared to me. Looking for some flip flops, I found my Nike slides. Slipping my feet inside, I grabbed my phone, keys and small wallet before running out the door. Ordering an Uber, I prayed it wasn't going to take long, the minute it gave me the car details and the amount of minutes, I pulled up my contacts. Scrolling to Saad's name, I let it ring as I tapped my foot impatiently against the pavement.

"Hey beautiful, why you up?"

"Saad, where the fuck are you? Like don't sit here and lie to me, matter fact FaceTime me." Ending the call, I tapped the camera button, Asaad dismissed the call and called me back.

"Lou what is wrong? Is the baby okay?"

Holding back the tears that were escaping, "Saad my daddy was shot, I don't know what's going on but I need to know that you're not mixed-up in this!" As I broke down in tears the Uber pulled up. Unable to control myself, the driver got out the car and asked if I was okay. Asaad was yelling into the phone asking who I was with and what was going on.

"Asaad Daniels, did you not hear what the fuck I said?" Now livid, I stood up wiping my face before climbing into the back of the car.

"Lou, I heard you and no I did not do that stupid shit. I'm out on bail; I'm not that dumb."

"So then, where are you?" Trying to calm my nerves down, I rolled down the window.

"I'm with Chinx right now, he had an emergency, so I rushed over here." Breathing into the line, he asked, "You good though? I'm sorry this is happening right now."

"No, I'm not good, like I can't stand him but I'm also not happy about the possibility of losing another parent."

"I understand, if you need me to come by, I'll swing by just to support you." Knowing he couldn't stand my father but agreed to come and be with me changed my mood. Letting him know I was good being alone right now but not to leave his phone on silent because I may need him. Ending the call, I climbed out of the car and headed straight to the emergency room. Giving the receptionist my father's name, she told me what ward he would be in.

Walking to the C ward, my heart began beating heavily. Trying to pace my breathing so I wouldn't go into a panic attack, my stomach started forming small knots. My nerves were shot, my hands were shaking and my eyes became glassy. Feeling my feet begin to drag as if I was moving bricks, everything seemed like it was moving in slow motion. Looking around for any sign of a nurse or doctor walking by, I spotted Gabby leaning up against the wall.

Snapping my neck, I walked directly up to her and asked her what she was doing here. She backed away before turning and walking away. Walking to go follow her, the nurse came out and asked who was there for Oliver Hinton. Raising my hand, she walked up to me and told me his condition.

"Is he your father?"

"Yes, I'm Lucy."

Touching the small of my back, she lead me to the chairs up against the wall, "He is alive, but he just went through extensive surgery to remove the bullets from his chest, shoulder and leg."

Gasping in shock, I hung my mouth open.

"We won't know how serious the damage is until he wakes up, but he did survive surgery."

Nodding my head, I took my hand from her hand and asked if I could see him. She led me to the room where he was laid up. Standing by the door, I looked in on him. He was laid up with a bandage on his shoulder. Blinking my eyes, I couldn't move.

My feet felt like cement bricks as I dragged them. Stepping beside his bedside, I shook my head in shame. "You're really too old to have your ass mixed up in this bullshit fa'real. I don't even know why you came out here." Looking at the machines that monitored his heart rate and blood pressure, I looked over his body. "You really out here getting shot at like you still a young dude, you're a whole fucking judge and soon to be grandfather!" Letting out my frustration, I was now shouting at him. Not sure if he could hear me or not, I spewed all the hatred I had towards him. "I'm not sorry I love Asaad and I'm not sorry I am having his child. I'm sorry you can't accept him and stop fucking chasing behind him because of your issues with his father and mommy." Shaking my head, I backed away from the bed, "I hope you pull through because I don't wish death on anyone but I want you to stay out of my life. Oh, and I'm sure Gabby being here wasn't a coincidence either." Turning on my heels, I left out of the room. Walking down the hallway, I allowed the tears to fall freely.

I wasn't crying because I was hurt, I was crying because I was letting go of the last parent I had. Walking, I nearly bumped into Gabby again, she turned her lip up at me and continued walking. Mentally, physically and emotionally drained, I charged it to the game. She was going to see me sooner or later and we shared the same baby father, so I'm sure it will be sooner than later. Getting on the elevator and riding in silence, I said a silent prayer. Once I was out of the hospital, I walked to the corner, allowing the wind to blow through my wild curls.

Looking down at my vibrating phone, Asaad was calling me. Sending him to voicemail, I texted him that I was over it and going home. He asked me was I okay, if I needed him or if he could do anything. I ignored every last message. Getting in a yellow cab, I ran off the address to the driver before laying my head back. Once I pulled up to the house, I expected Asaad to be there but he wasn't. Stripping out of the clothing I had on, I laid on the sofa snuggled under the throw blanket and Asaad's sweatshirt, massaging my temples trying to alleviate the oncoming headache.

"All of this shit is for the birds. This nigga always claiming I'm his fucking peace but the nigga was definitely my damn headache." Letting out an aspirated breath, I propped one of the throw pillows under my aching back closing my eyes and I was asleep.

36

ASAAD

Repeatedly texting Lou and calling her, I began to panic. Misha told me she was very stubborn when shit didn't go her way, but I didn't give a fuck. She was carrying my child and her father was just shot. I wasn't scared that the shooter was going to come after her because they weren't. I was mad that the shooter told me where they shot him. Hearing that he was coming out of my old house that I still owned with Gabby, I wanted to jump up and go strangle the bitch, but she wasn't worth it. I was already out on bail and I'd be damned if I jeopardized the little bit of time I had left with Lou before they found me guilty of something.

Pacing the floor, I kept looking down at my phone. Seeing no notifications pop up, I tried calling her again. "Listen Asaad, you're going to worry yourself sick. Lou is probably at the house by now."

"Misha, nah fuck that. What if she ran into that grimy bitch? And what the fuck was she doing with him anyway?"

"I don't know, but when I let them shots fire, her goofy ass sure came running out on some captain save a fucking hoe."

"I can't believe you really shot him though Misha." Taking the blunt from her hand, I took a toke from it.

"My baby cold," Chinx added, pulling Misha down into his lap. "The nigga better not survive cuz then I'ma have to go finish the job like I did with Hassel."

"Seeing the video and thinking about the letter, I wasn't about to let Oliver get off the hook."

"That's facts cuz my baby the little peaceful one," I added taking another drag from the blunt.

"You think she the peaceful one, she just pregnant and clearly not that upset, but trust me, Lou got my mother's blood running through her."

Throwing my head back in laughter, I replied, "Yeah, you ain't never lied."

"But on another note though, I gotta pay our father a visit because I still have some unanswered questions."

Raising my eyebrow at Misha, I knew she probably wanted to shoot my father too but I couldn't allow her to do that. "Nah you ain't shooting my pops. I know he pulled the trigger, but c'mon, he loved her."

"Oh nah, I'm not trying to kill him. I need to know some things about my mother from him."

Nodding at her, I passed Chinx the blunt before getting up to leave. "I'm 'bout to go check my baby and see if she's good."

Leaving out of the apartment, I jogged to my car. Starting it up, I tried calling Lou again. Giving up, I drove straight to the house. Unlocking the door, I walked in and spotted her on the sofa. Dropping my keys on the table by the door, I walked in. Bending down to her level, I planted a kiss on her forehead. She smiled before opening her eyes and looking at me.

"Baby I'm sorry about earlier. I should have dropped everything and came to you." Reaching her arms up to give me a hug, she told me it was okay. "It wasn't that okay because you ain't answer me." Scooting her over a little, I sat on the edge of the sofa.

"No, that was payback for your ass." Sitting up, she looked into my eyes before speaking.

"Asaad, I don't know how you're going to take this, but Gabby was with my father at the hospital and I'm sure she's the female who called me."

Already knowing that much, I shook my head acting as if it was news to me. "I think you should get a paternity test done on the baby."

"Yeah, I already had that in mind, but you think they're fucking around?"

Unsure of how much she knew about the relationship between the two, I wasn't about to be the one to bring her any bad news.

"I'm not sure, but I just think it's better to be safe than sorry."

"You're right, but c'mon. I wanna hold you and my big ass cannot fit on this couch with you and that belly." Laughing, she got up from the sofa with my help and wobbled to the room. I had noticed the new walk the other day and I found it to be the cutest shit. Unlike Gabby, I was excited about the baby Lou was carrying. Her skin was flawless and her hair was growing nice. Her breasts were no longer the small c-cup they were months ago; she was beginning to fill out.

Following her into the room, Lou walked around me before slightly pushing me onto the bed. Knowing her ass was horny all the time, I didn't even fight with her. Removing the oversized T-shirt she had on and her panties, I pulled off my clothing.

Strutting in my direction, she straddled me before sliding down on my dick. Throwing her head back, she loosened her walls to adjust to the size of my manhood. Placing her hands on my chest, she leaned forward before bouncing up and down on my dick. Hearing her moan in pleasure every time she came down on my dick sent me over the top. Lifting up her ass, I slammed her down on my dick, forgetting about her being pregnant.

"Argh, Asaad. Slow down baby, I'm about to cum." Hearing her tell me that, I got up carrying her and laid her on her back, continuing to fuck her. Her pussy contracted on my dick as her eyes laid low, biting her lip. I took her nipple in my mouth, she scratched at my back and neck. "Asaad, stop. You're killing me," she said through her panting. Ignoring her, I told her to take all of this dick. Slowing my pace, I hit her g-spot and walls. The minute she closed her eyes and a tear fell; I knew she was on her way to an orgasm.

Pumping in and out of her, Lou looked into my face. "Damn girl I love you."

"I love you, too, Asaad!" she cried out with her mouth open wide. Taking her tongue in my mouth, I released inside of her. Throwing my head forward, I pulled out before I crushed her small belly. Rolling over to my side, I laid on the bed trying to catch my breath.

"Asaad why do you always do me like that?" Lou asked in between taking heavy breaths. With her hand on her chest she chuckled. Getting up off the bed, she went to start the shower. Hearing the water turn on she was yelling from the bathroom.

"Girl, you know I can't hear your ass over that water!"

Getting up off the bed, I stepped into the bathroom to clean off the sex. Washing off before her, I left Lou there singing a Brian McKnight song she always sung. Grabbing a pair of basketball shorts and chuckling, I went to the kitchen to go and start a quick breakfast for her. Hearing my phone ringing, I grabbed it up without looking at the caller's number.

"Oh, you want to be big man now, huh? You really thought you were invincible?" Taking the phone from my ear, I looked down at Gabby's number. Rolling my eyes at her, I told her she was bugging before placing the phone back on my ear.

"Get the fuck off my line with this bullshit, Gabriella."

"Nah cuz, you think that you were going to shoot my nigga and get away with it, but newsflash he ain't dead!"

"Bitch you can have that wrinkled ass nigga's dick. My woman is more of a woman then you'll ever be, and while you at it hoe, she's about to have our baby."

"Fuck you Asaad, cuz if you forgot, I'm still married to your ass and also pregnant, so you will be taking care of me and my nigga baby."

Laughing, I had to catch myself before I choked. I couldn't believe this bitch had the audacity to think I was going to take care of a baby that I wasn't sure was mine. She kept rambling on and on as I cut on the water in the kitchen, blocking out half of her rant.

"Listen Gabby, while this might be cute for you, I got shit to do, so get the fuck off my line."

"Oh, before you go, you need to know I worked for Oliver and Hassel and gave him you're whole inside operation." Ending the call, I leaned my head back squinting my eyes. I couldn't believe what I had just heard. Gabby had been working for Oliver this whole time. Calling Chinx, his phone rang out until the voicemail picked up.

Calling Gabby back, she answered sounding like she was laughing. "Oh, I bet that got your attention, huh? Yeah, you heard me right. This whole time you and Chinx swore you were doing something by trying to set up Hassel. He's been working as Oliver's rat for months."

"Bitch, I'll kill you right now!" I spat at her, walking towards the stairs just as my front door came flying in.

"Don't move Asaad! Drop the phone and stay the fuck right there!" Someone shouted from behind me. Dropping the phone on the floor, it hit the tiled floors hard. Lou must have heard the noise because she came rushing down the stairs in nothing but an oversized Morehouse shirt. Pointing a gun at her, she stopped, grabbing her chest.

"Baby don't move, stay right there and y'all better not shoot my girlfriend!" Turning around with my hands in the air, I said, "Her father is a judge!"

"Yeah, muthafucka we know. That's how we know all about your little operation you been running for some time."

Lou looked like she wanted to break down, but I shook my head no and told her to be strong. "I love you ma, I'ma call you as soon as I get inside."

Standing with her hands in the air on the stairs, Lou shouted asking if she should reach out to my family.

"Yeah, call my parents and tell them I'm booked!" One of the officers grabbed me forcefully and yanked me out of the house in just basketball shorts and slippers. Hearing Lou let out a cry, I clenched my jaws.

They say karma always comes back around, whether it's with you or your children. I'm not sure if it was my karma or my father's karma, but she was definitely a bald headed bitch!

37

LOU

Watching the officers ransack the house, I stood out front trying to reach Asaad's parents. Pacing back and forth I waited for them to answer.

"Hello," his mother asked concerned.

"Hey Sharee. Umm, Asaad was arrested and the charges are serious and I'm scared and I'm worried!" I cried into the line just as I turned around and heard a familiar voice.

"Look at who we have here, pregnant and fucking the enemy!" I licked my bottom lip and flared my nose before placing a punch right in her face.

"Henrietta, now is not the time to fuck with me!" I shouted in frustration, trying to land another punch to her face. The officers rushed to pull me away from her. Kicking my feet, I popped her on her leg.

"Ms. Hinton, we are going to need you to calm down," the female officer mentioned to me when they pinned me up against the car. Hearing Henrietta shout in the distance, I tried breaking free again.

"Lucy, c'mon you're pregnant. Think about the baby." I'd

forgotten all about my growing bump. Sucking my teeth, I walked off in the opposite direction. Wanting to unleash my frustration on someone, Henrietta was the closest candidate and I couldn't get to her. Spacing out, I bit my bottom lip a little tasting the coat of raspberry lip gloss. Holding back the tears, balling my hand into a fist, and digging my nails into the palms of my hands, I paced the concrete. Kicking over the few rocks by my foot, I roll my eyes as I turned up my lip to my nose.

This was the worst time for my life to be crumbling. Assad was gone, and here I was being taunted by the devil herself. Staring off into the distance, a police officer snapped me back to reality, waving his hands in my face.

"Lucy, you have to come down for questioning." With furrowed brows, I snap my neck in his direction. I was lost. I could have sworn Assad told their asses I had nothing to do with the bullshit, but seeing the smirk plastered on Henrietta's face, I knew she was behind all of this madness.

"You've got to be fucking joking, right?"

"As a matter of fact, we're not, so we can do this the easy way or I can get a warrant." *What part of the game was this bullshit?* I left Hassel's ass to avoid all of this and now this nigga Assad got me knee deep in it.

"Officer, she's clearly not going to go willingly." Henrietta just had to add her two cents in, sending me over the edge. Before I could charge at her, the male officer hemmed me up. Looking directly in my face, he yanked my arm. Pulling back the door to the police car, he forced me in.

"I'ma let them know you manhandled a fucking pregnant woman, too!" Before I could finish going off, the door slammed shut in my face. Fighting back the tears, I threw my head against the ripped leather seat.

If they thought I was about to be a snitch for a nigga who ain't give a fuck about me, they could pack that shit up. What could they charge me with? A bitch was fighting for her life just like he was. It just so happened that I came out alive and he was six feet under.

To be continued...

AFTERWORD

Texting List

To stay up to date on new releases, plus get information on contests, sneak peeks, and more...

Text ColeHartSig to (855)231-5230

9 798618 901369